l'arrêt
de mort

death
sentence

DEATH SENTENCE

DEATH SENTENCE

Maurice Blanchot

translated by Lydia Davis

Station Hill

First English language edition.
Copyright © 1978 by Station Hill Press.
All rights reserved.

ACKNOWLEDGEMENTS

Originally published in French under the title *L'Arrêt de Mort.* Copyright © 1948 by Editions Gallimard.

Portions of this translation first appeared in the following publications: *Living Hand, The Georgia Review,* & *Curtains.*

Special thanks to the Literature Panel of the National Endowment for the Arts, a Federal agency in Washington, D.C., for partial support of this project; to the Literature Panel of the New York State Council on the Arts, whose grant to the Open Studio Print Shop constitutes indirect support of this publication; & to the Department of Labor, for support under the Comprehensive Employment & Training Act.

Station Hill Press
Publisher: George Quasha
Barrytown, New York 12507

Produced at the Open Studio Print Shop
Director: Patricia Nedds
187 East Market Street
Rhinebeck, New York 12572

LLCN 78-59907
ISBN 0-930794-04-4 (paperback edition)
ISBN 0-930794-05-2 (hardcover edition)

DEATH SENTENCE

These things happened to me in 1938. I feel the greatest uneasiness in speaking of them. I have already tried to put them into writing many times. If I have written books, it has been in the hope that they would put an end to it all. If I have written novels, they have come into being just as the words began to shrink back from the truth. I am not frightened of the truth. I am not afraid to tell a secret. But until now, words have been frailer and more cunning than I would have liked. I know this guile is a warning: it would be nobler to leave the truth in peace. It would be in the best interests of the truth to keep it hidden. But now I hope to be done with it soon. To be done with it is also noble and important.

Still, I must not forget that I once managed to put these things into writing. It was in 1940, during the last weeks of July or the first weeks of August. Inactive, in a state of lethargy, I wrote this story. But once it was written I reread it and destroyed the manuscript. Today I cannot even remember how long it was.

I will write freely, since I am sure that this story concerns no one but myself. It could actually be told in ten words. That is what makes it so awful. There are ten words to say. For nine years I have held out against them. But this morning, which is the 8th of October (I have just noticed to my surprise) and so nearly the anniversary of the first of those days, I am almost sure that the words which should not be written will be written. For many months now, I think, I have been resolved to do it.

There are several witnesses to what happened, although only one, the one in the best position to know, glimpsed the truth. I used to telephone the apartment where these things happened — often in the beginning, and then less often. I once even lived there, at 15, rue —. I think the young woman's sister remained there for some time. What became of her? She lived, as she liked to say, off the kindness of gentlemen. I assume she's dead.

Her sister had all the strength of will and all the force of life. Their family, of middle-class background, had failed rather miserably: the father had been killed in 1916; the mother, left in charge of a tanning factory, went bankrupt without realizing what was happening. She got married again, to a stock-breeder, and one day the two of them abandoned their separate enterprises and bought a winery on a street in the 15th arrondissement. Whatever money they still had must have been lost there. Theoretically, one part of the factory belonged to the two daughters, and there were often very heated arguments about money. It would be fair to say that over the years Mme. B. had spent a small fortune on the health of her older daughter, which she reproached her with in perfect thoughtlessness.

I have kept "living" proof of these events. But without me, this proof can prove nothing, and I hope no one will go near it in my lifetime. Once I am dead, it will represent only the shell of an enigma, and I hope those who love me will have the courage to destroy it, without trying to learn what it means. I will give more details about this later. If these details are not there, I beg them not to plunge unexpectedly into my few secrets, or read my letters if any are found, or look at my photographs if any turn up, or above all open what is closed; I ask them to destroy everything without knowing what they are destroying, in the ignorance and spontaneity of true affection.

Because of something I did, someone had a very vague suspicion of this "proof" towards the end of 1940. Since she knew almost nothing of the story, she was not even able to skim the truth of it. She only guessed that something was shut up in the closet. (I lived in a hotel then.) She saw the closet, and made a move to open it, but at that moment she was overcome by a strange attack. Falling on the bed, she began to tremble incessantly; all night long she trembled without saying anything; at dawn, she began breathing hoarsely. It went on for about an hour, then sleep overpowered her and gave her a chance to recover. (That person, who was still very young, had more good sense than sensitivity. Even she complained about her unfailing calm. But at that moment her rationality deserted her. I should add that although she had never had an attack before, it could have been the effect of an unsuccessful poisoning attempt two or three years earlier; sometimes poison is reawakened, stirred up, like a dream, in a body that has been very badly shaken.)

The principal dates should be found in a little notebook locked in my desk. The only date I can be sure of is the 13th of October—Wednesday, the 13th of October. But that is hardly important. Since September I had been living in Arcachon. It was during the Munich crisis. I knew she was as ill as anyone could be. I had stopped off in Paris at the beginning of September, as I was returning from a trip, and had gone to see her doctor. He gave her three more weeks to live. Yet she got up every day; she lived on equal terms with an exhausting fever, she shivered for hours, but in the end she overcame the fever. On the 5th or 6th of October, I think, she was still going for rides in the car with her sister, along the Champs Elysées.

Although she was several months older than I was, she had a very young face which the disease had hardly touched. It is true that she wore make-up, but without make-up she seemed even younger, she was almost too young, so that the main effect of the disease was to give her the features of an adolescent. Only her eyes, which were larger, blacker, and more brilliant than they should have been—and sometimes pushed from their sockets by the fever—had an abnormal fixity. In a photograph taken during September her eyes are so large and so serious that one must fight against their expression in order to see her smile, though her smile is very conspicuous.

After I spoke to the doctor, I told her, "He gives you another month."

"Well, I'll tell that to the queen mother, who doesn't believe I'm really ill."

I don't know whether she wanted to live or die. During the last few months, the disease she had been fighting for ten years had been making her life more limited every day, and now she cursed both the disease

4

and life itself with all the violence she could rouse. Some time before, she had thought seriously of killing herself. One evening I advised her to do it. That same evening, after listening to me, unable to talk because of her shortness of breath, but sitting up at her table like a healthy person, she wrote down several sentences that she wished to keep secret. I got these sentences from her, in the end, and I still have them. They consist of a few words of instruction: she asks her family to make the funeral as simple as possible and expressly forbids anyone to visit her grave; she also makes a small legacy to A., one of her friends, the sister-in-law of a fairly well-known dancer.

No mention of me. I can see how bitter she had felt when she heard me agree to her suicide. When I think it over carefully, as I did afterwards, I realize that this consent was hardly excusable, was even dishonest, since it vaguely rose from the thought that she should have been dead long ago, but not only was she not dead, she had continued to live, love, laugh, run around the city, like someone whom illness could not touch. Her doctor had told me that from 1936 on he had considered her dead. Of course the same doctor, who treated me several times, once told me, too, "Since you should have been dead two years ago, everything that remains of your life is a reprieve." He had just given me six more months to live and that was seven years ago. But he had an important reason for wishing me six feet underground. What he said only suggested what he wanted to happen. In J.'s case, though, I think he was telling the truth.

I hardly remember how the scene ended. It seems to me she meant to tear up the piece of paper. But as I gave it back to her I was seized by a great tenderness for her, a great admiration for her courage, for that cold and watchful look in the face of death. I can still see her at her table, silently writing those final and strange words. That tiny will, in keeping with her propertyless, already dispossessed existence, that last thought, from which I was excluded, touched me infinitely. In it I recognized her violence, her secrecy; I saw that she was at liberty to fight even me up to the last second. She cried often and for long stretches. But her tears were never the tears of a coward. During very violent scenes she hit me two or three times, and I should have stopped her, because as soon as she realized what she had done she was upset, almost terrified: terrified at having touched me and also at having done something mean, but even more at having to recognize her ungovernable excitement, against which I offered no defense. She felt punished by it, offended, and endangered. Yet if she had tried to kill me, I would no doubt have warded off her blows. I could not have caused her the sadness of killing me. A year or two earlier, a young woman had shot at me with a revolver, after vainly waiting for me to disarm her. But I did not love that young woman. As it happened, she killed herself some time after that.

So for these reasons I kept that piece of paper, and for the few strange words it contained. Suicide disappeared from her thoughts. The disease left her no more breathing space. In those days her sister did not live with her all the time. Or at least, leading the sort of life she did, she was often absent, and might or might not return home at night. J. had a cleaning woman who came at meal times, but during the holidays she did not come. So J. was often left alone. The concierge, who liked her fairly well, went up to see her. She had only a few friends, although in the past she had gone out frequently. Even A., whom she was glad to see, bored her. But she would have welcomed anyone, because when she was alone she was afraid. She was very brave, but she was afraid. She was always very afraid of the night. When I first met her, in a hotel where I was staying at the time, she was in a little room on the second floor and I was in a fairly large room on the third. I can't say I knew her, since I had only crossed her path and greeted her several times. But one night she wakened with a start and felt the presence of someone she took to be me standing at the foot of her bed; shortly afterwards she heard the door close and footsteps move away down the hall. Then she was suddenly convinced that I was about to die or had just died. She went up to my room, although she didn't know me, and called to me through the door. Without thinking, I answered, "Don't be afraid," but in a strange voice, more frightening than reassuring. She was still so frightened that she thought I really was dead, and pushed the door, which gave way and opened, though it had been locked. I was not at all sick, though perhaps a little worse than sick. Fairly frightened myself, I woke up. I swore to her that I had not been in her room, that I had not left my own. She stretched out on my bed and fell asleep almost immediately. Of course one could laugh at it, but it is in no way laughable, and the impulse which carried her towards an unknown man in the middle of the night, which left her at his mercy, was a noble impulse, and she acted on it in the most true and just manner. I know of only two people capable of doing a thing like that, and even then I can only be sure of one.

Fear and the disease together changed day into night

for her. I don't know what she was afraid of: not of dying, but of something more serious. She had the telephone within arm's reach and she could call the concierge without dialing. Her mother also came once or twice a week, but no sooner had she arrived than she would find an excuse for going away again. That behavior annoyed her. She reproached her mother, then reproached herself for having cried, for having worked herself up to the point of crying, over an incident which she found insignificant and over a person she did not like very much. But it seemed strange to her that even though her mother knew she was in near agony she would not give up, for her sake, the chance to go shopping. That is why she had been happy to learn about the doctor's prognosis: she was delighted at the idea of proving something to her mother. Her mother actually did moan and weep, but would not prolong her visit by even one minute. Every minute stolen from solitude and fear was an inestimable boon for J. She fought with all her strength for one single minute: not with supplications, but inwardly, though she did not wish to admit it. Children are that way: silently, with the fervor of hopeless desire, they give orders to the world, and sometimes the world obeys them. The sickness had made a child of J.; but her energy was too great, and she could not dissipate it in small things, but only in great things, the greatest things.

When I left for Arcachon it had been decided that J. would undergo a new treatment invented by a physicist from Lyons, a treatment that was not yet generally accepted and that appeared to be excellent for sick people who were not very sick, but was almost certain to kill anyone in a critical condition. It was because of the treatment that I had gone to see J.'s doctor. He calculated that there was an eighty percent risk that she would die. Without the treatment, the risk would become certainty—death in three weeks. I liked the idea of this treatment; I don't know why. J. liked it just as much. The doctor hesitated, but was in favor of administering it. I realized later that in many ways the doctor lacked good judgment. He had studied Paracelsus fairly seriously and devoted himself to conducting experiments that were sometimes outrageous and sometimes childish. We tried two or three together during the time I visited him, when he was hoping to get rid of me. He called himself a Catholic, he meant a practicing Catholic. The first day, he greeted me with this statement: "I am fortunate enough to have faith, I am a believer. What about you?" On the wall of his office there was an excellent photograph of the Turin Sudario, a photograph in which he saw two images superimposed on one another: one of Christ and one of Veronica; and as a matter of fact I distinctly saw, behind the figure of Christ, the features of a woman's face— extremely beautiful, even magnificent in its strangely proud expression. One last thing about this doctor: he was not without his good qualities; he was, it seems to me, a great deal more reliable in his diagnoses than most.

During the beginning of my stay in Arcachon, J. wrote to me at fairly great length, and her handwriting was still firm and vigorous. She told me the doctor had just had her sign a paper in case an accident should occur. So the treatment, which consisted of a series of shots—one each day, given to her at home—was about to begin. The evening before, she felt a violent, stabbing pain near her heart and had such a severe attack of choking that she telephoned her mother, who then called the doctor. This doctor, like all fairly prominent specialists, was not often willing to go out of his way. But this time he came quite quickly, no doubt because of the treatment he was supposed to begin administering the next day. I don't know what he saw: he never talked to me about it. To her, he said it was nothing, and it is true that the medicine he prescribed for her was insignificant. But even so, he decided to postpone the treatment several days.

The pain near her heart did not go away, but the symptoms died down and she had triumphed once more. The treatment was discussed again: she wanted it very much, either in order to get it over with or because her energy could no longer be satisfied with an uncertain objective—to live, to survive—but needed a firm decision on which she could lean heavily. Then a curious thing happened. I had sent a very beautiful cast of J.'s hands to a young man who was a professional palm reader and astrologer, and I had asked him to establish the greater coordinates of her fate. J.'s hands were small and she didn't like them; but their lines seemed to me altogether unusual—cross hatched, entangled, without the slightest apparent unity. I cannot describe them, although at this very moment I have them under my eyes and they are alive. Moreover, these lines grew blurred sometimes, then vanished, except for one deep central furrow that corresponded, I think, to what they call the line of fate. That line did not become distinct except at the moment when all the others were eclipsed; then, the palm of her hand was absolutely white and smooth, a real ivory palm, while the rest of the time the hatchings and the wrinkles made it seem almost old; but the deep hatchet-stroke still ran through the midst of the other lines, and if that line is indeed called the line of fate, I must say that its appearance made that fate seem tragic.

At that time the young man wrote to me: he said nothing about the hands. I think he challenged the exactness of the cast, although the impression had been taken by a sculptor about whom I will perhaps say something more. But in his astrological finding he described J.'s disease very exactly (I had naturally not told him about it) and announced that after a course of treatment she would be almost completely restored to health. His note ended with these words: she will not die. There were also some comments on J.'s character and on the general course of her destiny; that was left fairly vague. On the whole, the work was quite mediocre, and the only things that struck us were the few accurate details about the disease and, especially, the allusion to the treatment and its wonderful results. J. made fun of it. She was only a little superstitious, and only about unimportant things. In her nightly terror, she wasn't superstitious at all; she faced a very great danger, one that was nameless and formless, altogether indeterminate, and when she was alone she faced it all alone, without recourse to any tricks or charms. Sometimes she read her sister's cards. Her sister went the rounds of all the fortunetellers and tried to captivate prosperous-looking men in cafés (having the waiter bring them another drink). She succeeded once or twice.

The day appointed for the first injection of the treatment (which was supposed to bring on a long fainting fit in any case) was one of the darkest before the Munich crisis. Each morning during the preceding days the hotel manager announced to me that yet another guest, sometimes two, had left the hotel. But he was still somewhat hopeful, because a prominent political figure who had been staying at the hotel for a week had not left. But that day the man called for his car and left; dozens of others left after him. Large though it was, the hotel was already a desert. I ought to have left too, if only for the sake of my work, but I did not. Today I try without success to understand why I stayed away from Paris then, when everything was calling me back. The thought of that absence makes me uneasy, yet the reasons for it escape me. Mysterious as were the consequences of those events, it seems to me that my deliberate absence, which allowed them to happen, is even more mysterious. I knew that J. wanted to see me, and at such a time wanted to see no one but me, although she had told me just the opposite in order not to interrupt my peace and quiet. My newspaper paged me that day, twice, but I did not answer. I was waiting for a telephone call from J., or from her sister, but there wasn't one. I received no news the next day. It could be that I thought of going then, but that isn't certain. It is hard to find out the truth.

The day after that, I received a few words in J.'s hand, in her hand rather than her handwriting, since the handwriting was extraordinarily tortured. She told me that one hour before coming for the first injection, the doctor had decided to leave in order to get his children settled in the country; he would be back in a day or two. "Take cover behind your sandbags," the doctor told her on the telephone, making a stupid allusion to the home front's passive defense. "Well," said J.'s note at the end, "I will soon be even safer, six feet underground." That short letter was written in ink, but was, as I said, absolutely tortured. I had the impression that something in her was on the point of breaking, that in some very dark place inside her a battle was being fought that I was afraid of. For the first time I decided to telephone her. It was around noon. She was alone. I could hardly hear her, because after the first word or two she was overwhelmed by a violent fit of coughing and choking. For a few seconds I listened to this ragged, suffocated breathing; then she managed to say to me, "Hang up," and I hung up.

The following day's letter was written in pencil, but it was longer and more tranquil, perhaps too tranquil. As I had feared, the telephone call upset her greatly: she was tormented by not being able to talk and, even more, by allowing me to hear that coughing, which she had not been able to control, and she had made a foolish effort to silence herself and tell me to hang up; after that effort, she must have lost consciousness, and later found herself on the floor, astonished, she said, and convinced that she had become a very young child again. Clearly, the phrase "hang up" had nearly cost her her life. From then on she remained almost constantly in bed. I telephoned her once or twice more and she talked to me peacefully, saying over and over, with a certain insistence, that when she saw me again she would have some very interesting and remarkable things to tell me. This same assurance appears in one of her letters: "When you come here, I hope I will be able to talk; I am saving all my breath for that moment, when I will tell you many important things that I have to tell you."

In the meantime the doctor had come back. The Munich crisis had begun by then. Since she could not reasonably be expected to go out, the doctor went to her. He told her she had too much courage, that the moment had come to dispense with courage. The treatment was no longer discussed. As he left, he called J.'s sister Louise to the stairway and told her it was inhuman to let her sister suffer like this; that there was no more hope and that they would have to resort to drugs. Louise wrote me about that, even though writing was a big production for her; she said also that J. knew nothing about this conversation and that naturally it would make "the little kid," as she called her older sister, happy to see me again. The conversation on the stairway was soon reported to the patient, who mentioned it to me with astonishing satisfaction in one of her last letters: "So now we come to morphine," she said.

The doctor's decision might seem natural and justified. I think it was. For J. the battle took another form and became even more difficult. This was no longer an honest, open struggle against an enemy who frankly wanted to fight. The shots calmed her, but they were also meant to calm something in her that could not be calmed, a violent and rebellious assertion against a force which did not respect it. She had a horror of hypocritically sweet behavior, and the sudden sweetness of the disease took her by surprise, deceived her, to such a degree that while she had been lively and almost normal before, getting up and going outdoors, now, after very few injections—perhaps two or three—she fell into a state of prostration that transformed her into a dying person. The doctor himself was frightened by this, even though he had foreseen it. He discontinued the injections and even—a surprising thing—withdrew his prescription for them. A nurse was spending the nights close to J. now, and soon began spending both the days and the nights there. Though the patient was irritable by nature, and not very likeable, this nurse, who was fairly young, became attached to her; she was drawn by J.'s beauty, which at the time, it seems, had become extraordinary. It is well known that for an instant after dying, people who were once beautiful become young and beautiful again: the disease, the almost absurd sufferings, the unending struggle to breathe, not to breathe too much, to stop the bursts of coughing which at every attack nearly suffocated her, all that extravagant and ugly violence, which should have made her hideous, could do nothing to mar the perfectly beautiful and young (though somewhat hard) expression that illuminated her face. That is certainly strange. I thought her beauty came from the radiance of her eyes, which were tainted by the poison. But her eyes were almost always closed, or if they opened, they opened for a brief instant, with a rapidity that was actually disconcerting, and looked at the world, recognized it, and kept a sharp eye on it, as if taking it by surprise.

Having been denied morphine, the illness did everything in its power to have it given again. J. did not want to live only for the sake of living. She thought it absurd and even ridiculous to suffer, if things could be otherwise. Stoicism did not suit her, and she became furiously angry when the shots were discontinued. Then it was evident that she was not really sicker than she had been before. The doctor was helpless. At first he objected, but after a scene in which J. insulted him, he yielded to her will, which was as strong as his own. During that scene, J. said to him, "If you don't kill me, then you're a murderer." Later I came across a similar phrase, attributed to Kafka. Her sister, who would have been incapable of inventing something like that, reported it to me in that form and the doctor just about confirmed it. (He remembered her as saying, "If you don't kill me, you'll kill me.")

This time the effects of the morphine were altogether different. J. remained calm, or a little calmer, but the passivity, the calm, was only apparent. It was as though, after having been deceived by the hypocritical drug, she had put herself on her guard and, behind the appearance of sleep, in the depths of her repose, had maintained a vigilance, a penetrating gaze that left her enemy no hope of attacking her unawares. It was from this moment on that her face assumed the expression of beauty that was so striking. I think she enjoyed forcing death to greater honesty and greater truth. She condemned it to become noble.

I'm not very sure how those days were spent. I didn't ask very many questions. I could hardly talk about her. The only person who talked to me was the doctor, a person without tact, often ridiculous, and amazed by what he saw. He talked to me more than he should have, and I questioned him. The nurse wanted to confide in me too. (I think she was called Dangerue, or something like that.) Later she said an odd thing to me: "If you ever become very sick yourself, I would be happy to be sent for." I know that "the little kid" sometimes talked to her at night for quite a long time: she asked her to describe some of the suffering she had witnessed as a nurse; and she asked her, "Have you ever seen death?"

"I have seen dead people, Miss."

"No, death!" The nurse shook her head. "Well, soon you will see it."

Her friend A. wrote to me. The first few lines were dictated by J.: according to these words, she was almost well; don't worry about me, she said, don't worry. Then she had felt misgivings; not being strong enough to write, she had found it strange to write to me through a third person, and had asked her friend to abandon the letter, to forget it. But A. wrote me all that, she told me particularly that J. did not want to disturb my peace and quiet but that it was obvious she thought of nothing but my return, that all the other people annoyed her, jarred on her more and more, that soon she would not be able to stand anyone's presence, as long as I was absent. I think in saying that, she was announcing that she was going to die. This time I decided to return to Paris. But I gave myself two more days. I let her know by telephone or by telegram.

My official address in Paris was a hotel in rue d'O. I went there Monday evening (I've thought about that date and now I'm sure of it) on returning, quite tired out, from Arcachon. In the middle of the night, at two or three o'clock, the telephone woke me up. "Come, please come, J. is dying." The voice was Louise's. I didn't have far to go and I don't think I delayed. I was surprised to find the door of the apartment open. The apartment wasn't big, but it had a fairly large front hall, and in order to reach her room it was necessary to walk down a corridor. In the corridor I bumped into the doctor who was pleased to meet me, took me by the arm, with his usual lack of ceremony, and led me outside onto the landing. "My poor man." He nodded his head in a sinister way. I didn't hear anything he said until the shocking vulgarity of one phrase startled me: "It's a blessed release for the poor creatures." Once again he explained certain things which I don't remember very well: I think he tried to justify his decision to abandon the treatment. He also said, "What strength of will!" because barely half an hour before she had called him herself, working herself up to force him to come; he liked that last outburst. So, she had made him come at the last moment, and not me, she had spoken to him, and not to me. I looked at this great vulgar fellow, who was foolishly repeating, "I told you so; three weeks, exactly three weeks."

"It's been five weeks!" I said this rashly, provoked to exasperation by what he had said. But when I saw him so suddenly taken aback, I reconsidered what I had said, and it dawned on me that at a certain moment in the night she must have felt defeated, too weak to live until morning, when I would see her, and that she had asked the doctor's help in order to last a little longer, one minute longer, the one minute which she had so often demanded silently and in vain. This is what that poor fool mistook for anger, and doubtless he had given in to her by coming, but he was already too late: at a time when she could no longer do anything, he could do even less, and his only help had been to cooperate with that sweet and tranquil death he spoke of with such sickening familiarity. My grief began at that moment.

The room was full of strangers. I think her mother was there, her stepfather, and maybe another relative. All these people were strangers to me. The nurse, whom I didn't know, was there too. This gathering of strangers close to her silent body was what she would have found most unbearable. It was something incongruous which she should have been spared and which turned my grief to bitterness and disgust. I remained standing in front of her, but because of all those people I could not see her. I know I looked at her, stared at her, but did not see her. I could only speak to Louise, who was the only one who reminded me of her as she had been when she was alive, or rather Louise talked to me first:

I would have liked to understand why, after having resisted so stubbornly for so many interminable years, she had not found the strength to hold out for such a short time longer. Naively, I thought that interval had been a few minutes, and a few minutes was nothing. But for her those few minutes had been a lifetime, more than that eternity of life which they talk about, and hers had been lost then. What Louise said to me when she telephoned—"She is dying"—was true, was the kind of truth you perceive in a flash, she would die, she was almost dead, the wait had not begun at that moment; at that moment it had come to an end; or rather the last wait had gone on nearly the duration of the telephone call: at the beginning she was alive and lucid, watching all of Louise's movements; then still alive, but already sightless and without a sign of acceptance when Louise said, "She is dying"; and the receiver had hardly been hung up when her pulse, the nurse said, scattered like sand.

Louise did not have much presence of mind, nor much heart. But all of a sudden she must have read in my face that something was about to happen that she knew she did not have the right to see, nor anyone else in the world, and instantly she took them all away. I sat down on the edge of the bed, as I had done many times. She was a little more stretched out than I would have imagined; her head lay on a little cushion and because of that she had the stillness of a recumbent effigy and not of a living being. Her face was serious and even severe. Her lips, tightly pressed together, made me think of her violently clenched teeth which had shut at the last moment and even now did not relax. Her eyelids, too, were lowered. Her skin, strikingly white next to the black brilliance of her hair, wrung my heart.

She who had been absolutely alive was already no more than a statue. It was then that I looked at her hands. Fortunately they were not joined, but as they lay askew on the sheet, awkwardly clutched in a last contraction which slightly twisted the fingers, they seemed so little to me, so diminished by the clumsiness of their last effort, so much too weak for the immense battle which that great soul had fought, all alone, that for an instant I was overwhelmed by sadness. I leaned over her, I called to her by her first name; and immediately—I can say there wasn't a second's interval—a sort of breath came out of her compressed mouth, a sigh which little by little became a light, weak cry; almost at the same time—I'm sure of this—her arms moved, tried to rise. At that moment, her eyelids were still completely shut. But a second afterwards, perhaps two, they opened abruptly and they opened to reveal something terrible which I will not talk about, the most terrible look which a living being can receive, and I think that if I had shuddered at that instant, and if I had been afraid, everything would have been lost, but my tenderness was so great that I didn't even think about the strangeness of what was happening, which certainly seemed to me altogether natural because of that infinite movement which drew me towards her, and I took her in my arms, while her arms clasped me, and not only was she completely alive from that moment on, but perfectly natural, gay and almost completely recovered.

The first words she spoke, though, were somewhat distressing. In themselves they weren't; and now that I have just written that they were, I can't really understand why. "How long have you been here?" Those were the words she spoke almost immediately. It could be that I had just realized the strangeness of the situation, and something of that strangeness came through her words. But I believe her voice itself was still a little surprising; her voice was always surprising—fairly harsh, lightly veiled, clouded by disease and yet always very gay or very lively. But I think I was also struck by its uneasy inflection: as she asked me how long I had been there, it seemed to me she was remembering something, or that she was close to remembering it, and that at the same time she felt an apprehension that was linked to me, or my coming too late, or the fact that I had seen and taken by surprise something I shouldn't have seen. All that came to me through her voice. I don't know how I answered. Right away she relaxed and became absolutely human and real again.

Strange as it may seem, I don't think I gave one distinct thought, during that whole day, to the event which had allowed J. to talk to me and laugh with me again. It is simply that in those moments I loved her totally, and nothing else mattered. I only had enough self-control to go find the others and tell them J. had recovered. I don't know how they took the news; perhaps just as naturally as I did. I vaguely remember that they were huddled in the kitchen and in one of the other rooms and that, according to Louise, who reported it to me, they complained that I had treated them like intruders. I certainly didn't want to mistreat them. I had practically forgotten them, that's all. I remember that later I had Louise ask for authorization to have her sister embalmed. These practices were believed to be unhealthy, to say the least. But whatever impression fearfulness induced them to form of me, I can hardly hold it against them. I must even admit that given such unusual circumstances, these people showed admirable reserve, whether through ignorance or dread or for some other reason, and, in the end, behaved perfectly.

I recall few things worth mentioning about that day. J.'s waking took place at dawn, almost with the sunrise, and the dawn light charmed her. In terms of the illness itself—judging it as though it had followed its natural course—I found her much better than I would have imagined after everything that had been written to me, particularly after so many shots, which had been given to her every day. Apparently the morphine had not affected her spirits at all: someone who is saturated with drugs can seem lucid and even profound, but not cheerful; well, she was extremely and naturally cheerful; I remember that she poked fun at her mother in the kindest manner, which was unusual. When I think of all that took place before it and after it, the memory of that gaiety should be enough to kill a man. But at the time, I simply saw that she was gay, and I was gay too.

During that whole day she had almost no attacks, though she talked and laughed enough to bring on twenty. She ate much more than I did—although for many days she had been unable to eat anything—and her greatest worry was that I ate so little. She was somewhat uneasy because the nurse had taken advantage of my presence to spend the day at home. I noticed, then, a certain connivance between them which I had more evidence of later. She made fun of the doctor again and again. I asked her if she remembered telephoning him that night, if she knew he had come. "So he really came last night!" she said with an almost incredible expression of astonishment and discovery, but she did not ask me any questions. I asked her what those interesting things were that she had said she would talk to me about on my return. Then she had a sort of fit of absent-mindedness and distantly answered:

"Yes, when you come back I'll talk to you about it." One of her friends came that afternoon, a young woman originally from Constantinople. J. had spent many months with her but hardly saw her any more. The young woman must have learned that she was very sick, and came out of politeness to see how she was. I don't know what the others told her, but thinking that J. was near the end, she said to them that this was the time when the danger of contagion was greatest and that one shouldn't enter the room. Perhaps that is why they left me in peace: I don't know. She herself did not want to come in, and stuck her head through the half-open door, gesturing and making faces. "What's the matter with her?" J. asked me, suddenly irritated. "Do I frighten her? Am I that ugly?" The girl's behavior was all the more ridiculous because she had the same disease and was two steps away from the grave herself. J. asked for a mirror, looked at herself for a long time and said nothing. She was still very beautiful.

Towards evening she was no worse physically, but her mood had changed a little. I became uneasy too. I began to be aware of how exceptional this situation was. When I passed through Paris in September I had bought J. a big lamp, and she liked its lampshade, which was painted white. She had the lamp placed at the foot of the bed, directly in her line of vision, which must have bothered her, but she wanted it that way. Later, in the course of the night, when I saw that her eyes were fixed, riveted on the light, I suggested to her that it should be moved away or hidden; but she squeezed my wrist so tightly, to hold me back, that in the morning my skin was still white there. As soon as evening came she got the idea that I should leave. When I did not leave, when I did not return to my hotel, she worried about how tired I must be, and as the night advanced her worry turned into astonishment, a question about something mysterious and frightening which she did not press but returned to with greater and greater foreboding. At one point she stared at me with a penetration which makes me shiver now. "Why," she said coldly, "are you staying *precisely* tonight?" I suppose she was beginning to know as much as I did about the events of the early morning, but at that moment I was frightened at the thought that she might discover what had happened to her; it seemed to me that would be something absolutely terrifying for anyone to learn who was naturally afraid of the night. Perhaps I was wrong not to believe she had enough courage, just then, to face even the few things she had been afraid of before, because that night I did not see any fear in her, or if she was afraid, it was because she herself had become frightening. Perhaps I did commit a grave error in not telling her what she was waiting for me to tell her. My deviousness put us face to face like two creatures who were lying in wait for one another but who could no longer see one another.

My excuse is that in that hour I exalted her far above any sort of honesty, and the greatest truth mattered less to me than the slightest risk of worrying her. Another excuse is that little by little she seemed to approach a truth compared to which mine lost all interest. Towards eleven o'clock or midnight she began to have troubled dreams. Yet she was still awake, because I spoke to her and she answered me. She saw what she called "a perfect rose" move in the room. During the day I had ordered some flowers for her that were very red but already going to seed, and I'm not sure she liked them very much. She looked at them from time to time in a rather cold way. They had been put in the hall for the night, almost in front of her door, which remained open for some time. Then she saw something move across the room, at a certain height, as it seemed to me, and she called it "a perfect rose." I thought this dream image came to her from the flowers, which were perhaps disturbing her. So I closed the door. At that moment she really dozed off, into an almost calm sleep, and I was watching her live and sleep when all of a sudden she said with great anguish "Quick, a perfect rose," all the while continuing to sleep but now with a slight rattle. The nurse came and whispered to me that the night before that word had been the last she had pronounced: when she had seemed to be sunk in complete unconsciousness, she had abruptly awakened from her stupor to point to the oxygen balloon and murmur, "A perfect rose," and had immediately sunk again.

This story chilled me. I told myself that what had happened the night before, from which I had been excluded, was beginning all over again, and that J., drawn by some terrifying but perhaps also alluring and tempting thing, was reverting to those last minutes when the long wait for me had been too much for her. I think that was true. I even think that something was happening then that I found completely disheartening, because I took her hand gently, by the wrist (she was sleeping), and scarcely had I touched it when she sat up with her eyes open, looked at me furiously and pushed me away, saying, "Never touch me again." Then immediately she stretched out her arms to me, just as in the morning, and burst into tears. She cried, she sobbed against me in such a transport of grief that she was on the point of suffocating, and since the nurse had left the room in order not to witness this scene, I had to support her by myself without being able to get the oxygen balloon, which was just out of reach. While this was happening, the nurse came back and gave her the oxygen, which helped her to control herself. But after that she did not let me leave her bedside.

She fell asleep again. Her sleep had a strange way of dissolving in an instant, so that behind it she seemed to remain awake and to be grappling with serious matters there, in which I played perhaps a terrifying role. She had fallen asleep, her face wet with tears. Far from being spoiled by it, her youth seemed dazzling: only the very young and healthy can bear such a flood of tears that way; her youth made such an extraordinary impression on me that I completely forgot her illness, her awakening and the danger she was still in. A little later, however, her expression changed. Almost under my eyes, the tears had dried and the tear stains had disappeared; she became severe, and her slightly raised lips showed the contraction of her jaw and her tightly clenched teeth, and gave her a rather mean and suspicious look; her hand moved in mine to free itself, I wanted to release it, but she seized me again right away with a savage quickness in which there was nothing human. When the nurse came to talk to me—in a low voice and about nothing important—J. immediately awoke and said in a cold way, "I have my secrets with her too." She went back to sleep at once.

What the nurse told me was not altogether without importance. She told me that during the day she had telephoned the doctor to let him know about the patient's changed condition. The doctor had cried, "Oh, good heavens!" That is all the nurse ever dared to tell me about it. J. had been given one shot early in the evening. At two or three o'clock, I became convinced that the same terrible thing that had happened the day before was in danger of repeating itself. It is true that J. did not wake up again. The nurse must have dozed off too. As I listened without pause to her slight breathing, faced by the silence of the night, I felt extremely helpless and miserable just because of the miracle that I had brought about. Then, for the first time, I had a thought that came back to me later and in the end won out. While I was still in that state of mind—it must have been about three o'clock—J. woke up without moving at all—that is, she looked at me. That look was very human: I don't mean affectionate or kind, since it was neither; but it wasn't cold or marked by the forces of this night. It seemed to understand me profoundly; that is why I found it friendly, though it was at the same time terribly sad. "Well," she said, "you've made a fine mess of things." She looked at me again without smiling at all, as she might have smiled, as I afterwards hoped she had, but I think my expression did not invite a smile. Besides, that look did not last very long.

Even though her eyelids were lowered, I am convinced that from then on she lay awake; she lay awake because the danger was too great, or for some other reason; but she purposely kept herself at the edge of consciousness, manifesting a calm, and an alertness in that calm, that was very unlike her tension of a short time before. What proved to me that she was not asleep—though she was unaware of what went on around her because something else held her interest— was that a little later she remembered what had happened nearly an hour before: the nurse, not sure whether or not she was asleep, had leaned over her and suggested she have another shot, a suggestion which she did not seem to be at all aware of. But a little later she said to the nurse, "No, no shot this evening," and repeated insistently, "No more shots." Words which I have all the time in the world to remember now. Then she turned slightly towards the nurse and said in a tranquil tone, "Now then, take a good look at death," and pointed her finger at me. She said this in a very tranquil and almost friendly way, but without smiling.

Now I want to pass rapidly over all that happened. I have said more about it than I would have believed, but I am also touching the limit of what I can say. After she spoke about me as I have described, there was nothing extraordinary in her behavior, and the night ended rather quickly. Towards six o'clock she was sleeping deeply and almost like a healthy person. I arranged things with the nurse so that I could return to the hotel, where I stayed about an hour, and when I came back, Louise told me that she was still the same. But I saw right away that her condition had changed a good deal: the death rattle had begun and her face was the face of a dying person; besides that, her mouth was almost open, which had never happened to her at any time before while she was sleeping, and that mouth, open to the noise of agony, did not seem to belong to her, it seemed to be the mouth of someone I didn't know, someone irredeemably condemned, or even dead. The nurse agreed with me that things had gotten worse, but even so she asked my permission to see another patient and stop off at home, to be gone until the beginning of the afternoon. She thought the doctor would come during the morning, she also thought J. might sleep for many hours, during which one could only wait, without doing anything useful; she pointed out that her pulse was steady and holding up well.

The rattling became so loud and so intense that it

could be heard outside the apartment with all the doors closed. The comings and goings in the room seemed completely foreign to the unconscious body, itself a stranger to its own agony. Louise exasperated me a great deal, because the noise frightened her, and her mother also began to come in and make remarks, so that I didn't know where I was and began to hate the whole world; I no longer had any real feelings, not even for J., whose body was half dead and half alive. It could be that I drove these people away or that I went out for a moment (on the landing there was an armchair, and I sat down in it, where I could hear the rasping breath of her coma). What I'm sure of is that at one point during the morning, when I came back, I found J. awake again and feeling very bad. "You've come early," she said to me, and I saw that she had forgotten I had been there all night long. She was intensely annoyed because the nurse was not there. She called Louise, who ordinarily amused her but whose presence she could not bear for very long at a time. Extreme impatience rose from her whole being. If at first I was a little hurt by her coldness towards me, that did not last; I sensed too clearly the reason for that impatience, for that fever, for the surging of all her strength; I saw how, by a quicker movement than anything we could do, she kept one step ahead of the blows that were trying to do away with her. We were all very slow creatures and she needed to move like lightning to save her last breath, to escape the final immobility. I never saw her more alive, nor more lucid. Maybe she was in the last instant of her agony, but even though she was incredibly beset by suffering, exhaustion and death, she seemed so alive to me that once again I was convinced that if she didn't want it, and if I didn't want it, nothing would ever get the better of her. While attack followed attack—but there was no more trace of coma nor any fatal symptoms—when the others were out of the room, her hand which was twitching on mine suddenly controlled itself and clasped mine with the greatest impatience and with all the affection and all the tenderness it could. At the same time she smiled at me in a natural way, even with amusement. Immediately afterwards she said to me in a low and rapid voice, "Quick, a shot." (She had not asked for one during the night.) I took a large syringe, in it I mixed two doses of morphine and two of a sedative, four doses altogether of narcotics. The liquid was fairly slow in penetrating, but since she saw what I was doing she remained very calm. She did not move at any moment. Two or three minutes later, her pulse became irregular, it beat violently, stopped, then began to beat again, heavily, only to stop again, this happened many times, finally it became extremely rapid and light, and "scattered like sand."

I have no better way of describing it. I could say that during those moments J. continued to look at me with the same affectionate and willing look and that this look is still there, but unfortunately I'm not sure of that. As for the rest, I don't want to say anything. The difficulties with the doctor became a matter of indifference to me. I myself see nothing important in the fact that this young woman was dead, and returned to life at my bidding, but I see an astounding miracle in her fortitude, in her energy, which was great enough to make death powerless as long as she wanted. One thing must be understood: I have said nothing extraordinary or even surprising. What is extraordinary begins at the moment I stop. But I am no longer able to speak of it.

I will go on with this story, but now I will take some precautions. I am not taking these precautions in order to cast a veil over the truth. The truth will be told, everything of importance that happened will be told. But not everything has yet happened.

After a week of silence I have seen clearly that if I was expressing badly what I was trying to express, there would not only be no end, but I would be glad that there was no end. Even now, I am not sure that I am any more free than I was at the moment when I was not speaking. It may be that I am entirely mistaken. It may be that all these words are a curtain behind which what happened will never stop happening. The unfortunate thing is that after having waited for so many years, during which silence, immobility, and patience carried to the point of inertia did not for one single day stop deceiving me, I had to open my eyes all at once and allow myself to be tempted by a splendid thought, which I am trying in vain to bring to its knees.

Perhaps these precautions will not be precautions.

For some time I lived with a person who was obsessed by the idea of my death. I had said to her: "I think that at certain moments you would like to kill me. You shouldn't resist that desire. I'm going to write down on a piece of paper that if you kill me you will be doing what is best." But a thought is not exactly a person, even if it lives and acts like one. A thought demands a loyalty which makes any slyness difficult. Sometimes it is itself false, but behind this lie I still recognize something real, which I cannot betray.

Its uprightness is what actually fascinates me. When this thought appears, memory is no longer present, nor uneasiness, nor weariness, nor forboding, nor any recalling of yesterday, nor any plan for tomorrow. It appears, and perhaps it has appeared a thousand times, ten thousand times. What, then, could be more familiar to me? But familiarity is just what has disappeared forever between us. I look at it. It lives with me. It is in my house. Sometimes it begins to eat; sometimes, though rarely, it sleeps next to me. And I, a madman, fold my hands and let it eat its own flesh.

After these events, several of which I have recounted —but I am still recounting them now—I was immediately warned (told everything) about what was in store for me. The only difference, and it was a large one, was that I was living in proud intimacy with terror; I was too shallow to see the misery and worthlessness of this intimacy, and I did not understand that it would demand something of me that a man cannot give. My only strong point was my silence. Such a great silence seems incredible to me when I think about it, not a virtue, because it in no way occurred to me to talk, but precisely that the silence never said to itself: be careful, there is something here which you owe me an explanation for, the fact that neither my memory, nor my daily life, nor my work, nor my actions, nor my spoken words, nor the words which come from my fingertips ever alluded directly or indirectly to the thing which my whole person was physically engrossed in. I cannot understand this reserve, and I who am now speaking turn bitterly towards those silent days, those silent years, as towards an inaccessible, unreal country, closed off from everyone, and most of all from myself, yet where I have lived during a large part of my life, without exertion, without desire, by a mystery which astonishes me now.

I have lost silence, and the regret I feel over that is immeasurable. I cannot describe the pain that invades a man once he has begun to speak. It is a motionless pain, that is itself pledged to muteness; because of it, the unbreathable is the element I breathe. I have shut myself up in a room, alone, there is no one in the house, almost no one outside, but this solitude has itself begun to speak, and I must in turn speak about this speaking solitude, not in derision, but because a greater solitude hovers above it, and above that solitude, another still greater, and each, taking the spoken word in order to smother it and silence it, instead echoes it to infinity, and infinity becomes its echo.

Someone has said to me, with some annoyance, "In your presence, mouths open." That is possible, although it seems to me true of only a few people, because I have heard very few. But as I have listened to those few, my attention has been so great that they have not been able to be angry with me for what they said, nor reproach themselves with it, nor perhaps remember it. And I have always been more closely bound to them by what they have said to me than by what they could have hidden from me. People who are silent do not seem admirable to me because of that, nor yet less friendly. The ones who speak, or at least who speak to me because I have asked them a question, often seem to me the most silent, either because they evoke silence in me, or because, knowingly or unknowingly, they shut themselves up with me in an enclosed place where the person who questions them allies them with answers that their mouths do not hear.

I want to say, then, that "to have lost silence" does not at all mean what one might think. Besides, it hardly matters. I have decided to take this path. I still lived in the hotel in rue d'O. My room was small, and not very agreeable, but it suited me. In the next room lived a young woman who told me one day, when I made the mistake of speaking to her—she was on her balcony and I was on mine—that I annoyed her because I did not make enough noise. I think I actually did annoy her. In any case I did not disturb her very often, since I was rarely at home because of my work and even at night did not always return. This woman was on the point of breaking off relations with a friend of hers, a businessman from the Avenue de l'Opéra, who made her come to Paris two or three times a year, since she lived in the provinces, in Nantes or Rennes, I no longer remember which. She was married, with two children, and on top of that taught in a private girls' school. I do not know how she managed to fulfill all these obligations at once. Maybe that was pure make-believe. I am reporting these details, which do not interest me, as a way of getting started. I am deliberately trying to cast a spell over myself. And anyway, who can say what is important? This woman had a mingling of freedom and constraint in her character. It was clear that she was making a play for me. One evening when I came home, after having worked hard and with my mind on something else, I went to the wrong door and found myself in her room. There was certainly nothing intentional in this absent-mindedness. We both lived on the fifth or sixth floor, and the lights on that floor did not work. It is true that sometimes as I was coming home, the idea would occur to me that I might easily enter the wrong room, but I thought about it without hoping it would happen; I often did not even remember who lived there. For several minutes she reacted quite well to my presence. I suppose that was because she was wearing a beautiful dressing-gown. Even though it was nearly midnight, she was sitting in her armchair looking perfectly neat and presentable. That fact must have made everything else pleasant for her. Since she seemed quite pretty to me that day, I too thought my error meant something, and I did not tell her I had come in by mistake. Later on, she annoyed me very much. She was always wanting to come into my room and I did not want that. But she taught me something that I would not perhaps have discovered until much later if it had not been for her.

That day, something happened. I remember that she showed me her hand and said, "Look at this scar." On the back of her hand there was a rather large, diagonal swelling. Shortly afterwards I noticed that her mood had changed: a sort of cold respectability was mounting in her face, the sort of moral look which makes even the most beautiful face tiresome, and hers was only slightly pretty. I immediately wanted to leave. At that moment I must have told her I had come in by mistake, but she understood me to say I had made a mistake in coming in, which was something slightly different.

I have just been thinking about her. I realize that though I apparently behaved more or less the way anyone else would have, there must have been something absolutely offensive about my behavior that often made me her enemy. I suppose part of what she told me was true. I asked her questions about history, grammar, and botany, and she knew volumes about them. The only happy moments she spent with me were those hours of recitation, when she delivered entire chapters of Larive-et-Fleury and Malet to me. It relaxed me to listen to her. This knowledge, so incredibly old, soared over me croaking a kind of message which was always the same, and which more or less amounted to this: there is a time for learning, a time for being ignorant, a time for understanding, and a time for forgetting.

During these moments her face had a rather delicate expression. But it is certainly true that the other expression, which came over her unexpectedly and made me want to leave, might very well have been provoked by my attitude, since I behaved in a foolish way, and even if she did not see that clearly, the propriety of her distant past told her something about it from time to time and rose into her face again, where it looked out at me. I see it at this moment, that distant and ambiguous past which was certainly something ugly. But I do not know what I could have been or done to make her defend herself with an expression like that.

This scene appears to me now: I was in the metro. I think I was on my way home. By chance, I found myself sitting across from someone I knew. She told me she was married or about to be married. After one or two stops, she got off. This encounter reminded me of my neighbor C(olette). Suddenly I had the extraordinary impression that I had completely forgotten this woman, whom I saw almost every day, and that in order to remember her I had to seek out someone I had only glimpsed ten years before. If it had not been for that recent encounter, I not only would have lost sight of her altogether, but already, where she had been, there was a kind of immense, impersonal, though animate hole, a sort of living gap, which she emerged from only with difficulty. What complicated this impression was that the forgetting did not seem to be that. I saw her very clearly at that moment, and I would have seen her before, too, if I had thought of it. But on the other hand, I had to ask myself this: during the whole evening, yesterday, when she was there, did I notice her?

This ride on the metro left me with the recollection of a great sadness. The sadness had nothing to do with my short memory. But something profoundly sad was happening there in that car, with all those people going home to lunch. Very close to me was a great unhappiness, as silent as a real unhappiness can be, beyond all help, unknown, and which nothing could cause to appear. And I, as I felt this, was like a traveller walking on a road in the middle of nowhere; the road has summoned him and he walks onward, but the road wants to see if the man who is coming is really the one who should be coming: it turns around to see who he is, and in one somersault they both tumble into the ravine. Unhappy is the path that turns around to look at the man walking on it; and how much more profound was this unhappiness, how much more enigmatic and silent. At the hotel I left the concierge instructions not to disturb me, and gave her the key to my room to hang back up on the board, showing that I was not in. At about five o'clock someone entered the room without knocking. No one had ever dared come there before except the hotel employees and sometimes my brother.

Perhaps I could say why I would have walked a great distance when I had to see someone, though I hate to walk, rather than meet that person within the four walls of this hotel. There was nothing secret here. And besides, a few people always came to where I lived, and some of them came very often. There are quite natural reasons for it: the bother, when people come, of having to see them and hear them long after they have left; the need to make the place where one lives a place where nothing happens, which is why one can be at peace there, and also to make it a vacant place, where people who should not meet do not meet; and finally it is a test, because sooner or later a person who has been asked to stay outside will come there or prowl around nearby, so that at that point one discovers if it is a terrible fault or, quite the opposite, an agreeable thing. All these reasons seem good to me, but naturally they have their bad aspects. Yet there was still one other.

I was stretched out on my bed. It must have been very dark already. There was still a little light, I think, but since the curtains were not drawn, that light could have come from the street. The person who had entered was standing in the middle of the room. I was going to write that she was like a statue, because she was motionless and turned towards the window, and she really did have the look of a statue; but stone was not part of her element; rather, her nature was composed of fear—not an insane or monstrous fear, but one expressed by these words: for her, something irremediable had happened. I once saw a squirrel get caught in a cage that hung from a tree: he leaped across the threshold with all the energy of his very happy life, but hardly had he touched the planks inside when the light trigger clapped the door shut, and even though he had not been hurt, even though he was still free, since the cage was enormous, with a little pile of shells inside, his leap broke off abruptly and he remained paralyzed, struck in the back by the certainty that now the trap had caught him.

The strange thing was that she did not look at me or at anything else in the room. I might have thought she was trying to find the dim light from the window, that she had only come in for that last bit of daylight which fascinated her, sustained her, paralyzed her; but it was so faint that it could not have reached her eyes anyway, and once she had entered, inexplicably, she had only just enough strength left to remain standing in that room without dissolving into thin air. I think I was fairly calm. There are many things I could say about the impression I had, but I have the same impression now, as I look at that same person, who is standing several feet away from the window, just in front of the table, with her back to me; it is about the same time of day, she has come in and she is walking forward. (The room is different.) As I see her this way now, when she is no longer a surprise to me, I experience a much greater shock, a feeling of dizziness and confusion that I never had then, but something cold too, a strange pang, so much so that I would like to beg her to go back and stay behind the door, so that I could go out too. But this is the rule, and there is no way to free oneself of it: as soon as the thought has arisen, it must be followed to the very end.

I think I noticed only one thing: that she had a black, tailored suit on and wore no hat (which was more uncommon then than it is now); I could hardly see her hair, which I thought was much longer than people usually wore it, and because she was bowing her head she looked as though she had been struck or was expecting to be struck. What happened next shows how far she had already slipped outside the normal order of things. As she was turning around, she bumped into the table, and it made a noise. She reacted to the noise with a frightened laugh, and fled like an arrow. Then everything becomes confused. I think that after she cried out I grew wild. I saw her lunge toward the free air, and the instinct of the hunter seized me. I caught up with her near the stairway, grabbed her around the waist, and brought her back, dragging her along the floor as far as the bed, where she collapsed. My fit of rage was one of the few I have had since my very angry childhood, and it was uncontrollable. I do not know where this violence came from; I could have done anything at a time like that: broken her arm, crushed her skull, or even driven my own forehead into the wall, since I do not think this furious energy was directed at her in particular. Like the blast of an earthquake, it was an aimless force which shook people and knocked them over. I have been shaken by this blast too, and so have become a tempest which opens mountains and maddens the sea.

When the light was turned on, she did not seem to remember that tempest very clearly. "I must have fallen down," she said, examining her stockings. She was very surprised to see me out of breath and, I think, still wild-eyed. But it was the way I looked that little by little reminded her of something, doubtless not of what had happened, but of her own presence there, her footsteps in the street, this room that she was not familiar with, and—then what? Again she was driven toward the door.

One of the funny things about this scene was that although she had overcome many obstacles to arrive at this place, she now thought only of leaving, while I was holding her back not only against her will but also against my own. I should make it clear that she regarded me as someone she had apparently never seen before, that she therefore found herself shut up in a gloomy hotel room, completely disheveled, with a wild man who was throwing himself at her to stop her from making the slightest movement. And I was behaving in an entirely instinctual way too, for I had not realized that I did not know her, and was brutally pushing her back into the room not in order to keep her there, but to prevent her from going outside and losing that feeling of terror which she had found there and which obliged her to control herself or disappear.

Though the circumstances surrounding this encounter became easier to explain later, they were never any clearer than they were at that moment. N(athalie)'s character complicated them even further. One day I asked her, "What made you think of coming?" By then, I had met her four or five times in an office. She answered, "I've forgotten," and I think it was true. She was also extremely shy, though capable of unreasonable behavior. For instance she lost her way quite often in Paris, and though her shyness did not stop her from going up to people, it drove what she wanted to ask them from her mind, or, if she remembered, it made her forget the answer they gave her. She could look someone up that she did not know, if she had to, but if she knew him at all, the errand became more difficult, and if she knew that he found it annoying to have visitors, it became unbelievably difficult. That day was a Saturday, and she did not have to go to work; but she had a little girl, and she ought to have been with her then; and even if the lateness of the hour clearly did not stop her from going into the hotel, there were a thousand chances that she would get lost in the streets, since she saw very poorly at night.

She told me about it long afterwards—and she remained convinced that I never knew who she was, and yet treated her not like a stranger but like someone who was all too familiar. That was why she nearly went crazy herself: she could not face the immense task of making herself known to a man who was looking at her that way—with eyes in which she could not see herself —and saying to him: you met me at such-and-such a place. That seemed impossible to her. But since at the same time I was behaving with a sort of savage intimacy towards her—and not in the least as though she were a stranger—she was forced to believe that something had happened which she had not noticed, and that actually she was perfectly known to me, even if it meant she was someone she herself did not know. She repeated this to me, or to be more exact she told it to me when I insisted, after she had inadvertently begun a sentence which I had great trouble making her finish because I had spoken to her in a familiar way and also because she thought she should not have heard what I said. At one point I had said to her: "You're crazy, why did you go out today?" When she got home she remembered these words and as soon as she took them in she was extra-ordinarily happy (whereas her adventure had left a nightmarish feeling), but also convinced that she had just performed an act of madness that her inexperience and thoughtlessness made even more terrible. So she wanted to disappear completely, and after that I got nothing more from her.

This is the picture I have of the rest of the evening. After she left, I again began thinking about the girl who had told me, that morning, that she was going to be married. She worked in a bank; I knew where she lived, in a very nearby street, rue M. (Twice afterwards, it happened that I almost lived there.) I went to that building, where a political bi-weekly also had its offices in those days. On the stairway—the house is old and dilapidated, but the stairway is imposing—a cold draft passed over my shoulders, I felt tired, and I cursed the impulse that had brought me there. What was more, I could not remember exactly where the apartment was, I knocked or rang at several doors, and when no one answered I pushed against one of them without meaning to. Well, the door opened, which frightened me a little, and it opened on an unlighted area (the light in the stairwell having just gone out) which frightened me very much, because I thought I was in the wrong apartment. I had only been in that apartment a few times before; it was a single room, without an entryway, divided in two by a large curtain, with one side for the day, the other for the night. I can say now how I had come to know this young woman. She had been married before, and because of a lung disease, her husband had spent several years in a place where I was spending several weeks. I had seen her there. Six years later I saw her again, through a store window. When someone who has disappeared completely is suddenly there, in front of you, behind a pane of glass, that person becomes the most powerful sort of figure (unless it upsets you). For thirty seconds S(imone) D. gave me great pleasure, pleasure that was in some ways even immoderate and absurd, and because of those thirty seconds I was much friendlier to her than I ever would have thought of being. She had many good qualities, as far as I can judge; she was simple, and courageous, accepted nothing from her wealthy in-laws, and was firm in a way that made her a good, healthy person—but she also had a tendency to be so honest that she was sometimes brutal: otherwise, it seems to me she behaved in a normal way. The truth is that after I had been fortunate enough to see her once through a pane of glass, the only thing I wanted, during the whole time I knew her, was to feel that "great pleasure" again through her, and also to break the glass. As she came out of the store, and as soon as she recognized me, the first thing she said was, "You know, Simon is dead" (their names were almost identical), "don't ever speak of him to me." She was certainly very attached to him; what she said was proof of it.

To come at this time of night, without warning, when she might have gotten married again, was the last thing she could have expected from me. It is possible that I was about to go back out, but I do not really think so, and that gloomy and unfamiliar room fascinates me now; my objective was certainly there, in the dark. When I think about the strangeness of what I was doing, I can see a reason for it: I too had opened a door, and was inexplicably entering a place where no one expected me; at least that reason occurred to me, as I looked at the darkness. But if I had wanted to know just how the madness of a short time before was going to start up again, and how a wild man might throw himself at me and how I myself might become a figure of terror, I was mistaken. Behind the curtain a small light was turned on. I recognized the room immediately. Shortly afterwards I felt the draft in the stairway again: I think I went straight back to the hotel.

At first S. had been rather glum, but she had grown more cheerful when she heard that I was not sure I would not find her married again. The ridiculous aspect of this situation drove away her bad mood. As I was leaving, I thought—and I must make it clear that it was a sad thought—that any man who is by himself can always go into the home of a young woman who is alone (and the opposite too, of course), without any difficulty and at any time of night, as long as he does not have too many reasons for going there. But in my room everything was quite different. Besides having the good qualities I described Simone D. was also honest but reserved. Later I understood that my sudden appearance in the night had actually made her extremely uncomfortable: it was obvious that for her this visitor, who should not have been there, evoked someone who belonged there. That is why she grew more cheerful when I told her I had expected to find her married. That showed her I was not too concerned about the past. But she was left with one doubt, and since she was so very honest she came to find me the next day in the restaurant where I ate, and said to me right away: "You don't approve of my marriage. That's why you came to see me last night." She was the sort of person to whom marriage means something, and though I said to her, "But marriage is not very important," she persisted in the idea that by getting married she was doing away with the past, when a dozen love affairs would have left it intact. She explained to me at length all the reasons she had for getting married. When someone starts in on the "reasons," he soon gets tripped up if he is at all honest, because he has too many reasons, and just one would be enough. Also, as I listened to her I discovered how much her marriage really had bothered me, not for my own sake, of course, and not even for the sake of the dead S., whom I did not remember, but because I had had a foreboding that some secret treachery was going to take place, one of those harrowing events which no one knows anything about, which begin in darkness and end in silence, and against which obscure misery has no weapon.

I would like to say something else now. I am talking about things which seem negligible, and I am ignoring public events. These events were very important and they occupied my attention all the time. But now they are rotting away, their story is dead, and the hours and the life which were then mine are dead too. What is eloquent is the passing moment and the moment that will come after it. The shadow of yesterday's world is still pleasant for people who take refuge in it, but it will fade. And the world of the future is already falling in an avalanche on the memory of the past.

In the end, I strongly urged her to get married. "Alright," she said, "fine. But I want to make it very clear that we're not going to see each other again." Then she sent me a letter which said, "If you can give me any explanation, no matter what it is, of why you came the other evening, then give it to me (in a letter)." But I did not answer. It was already the middle of winter. I became ill. The room I have been talking about was extremely warm; an enormous, burning hot pipe ran alongside the bed to feed into the radiator, so that when the radiator was turned off the room was no hotter or colder. It is difficult to express how much I needed that heat, which was killing me. When at night the temperature fell to 76 or 77 degrees (in the daytime it rose to 86), I would become uneasy. I really felt the cold, and this cold paralyzed me as it entered my blood.

Later, like many other people, I knew the power of cold. But even at the hardest moments, when the only warmth was in ice, I never had the sense of absolute cold which that 76 degrees gave me. Especially at night, the sort of winter that formed around me had a disconcerting effect, because I felt it just as much when I was asleep, and it mingled with my sleep, from which I broke free again and again, frozen and with frost on my lips.

During this illness, the director of one of the publications where I worked came to see me, and I could not tactfully prevent him from coming in. The same events that I am not talking about were driving him crazy. Since he bored me, I did not say a word; he thought I was nearing my end, he telephoned the doctor, who also gave me up for lost every few weeks, and got this opinion from him: "X? My dear sir, it's about time we raised a cross over him." A few days later, the doctor told me this as though it were an excellent joke. I do not want to dwell on these medical complications. To describe them in a few words, it happened that while the doctor was treating me for an ordinary lung disease he caused a change in my blood by injecting me with something he claimed to have invented: my blood became prematurely "atomic," which meant that it fluctuated in the same way it would have under the influence of radiation. I rapidly lost three quarters of my white blood cells and became frighteningly ill. The doctor put me in his clinic; he thought I was dying. But after two days of a peculiar struggle, I pulled through and he quickly took me home again, where my absence had gone unnoticed.

I will add just a few more words: I promised the doctor I would be silent and I am holding to that silence, by and large. He swore that what he had done was done on purpose, and was not the result of a blunder, and he gave me the reasons for it. That is possible. But his vanity was very great and might have induced him to confess to a crime sooner than admit he had made a mistake. In the end, the result was the same — he caused my blood to become mysterious, and so unstable that it was astonishing to analyze.

Either because of my weakness after that experience, or because one does not always think about the things that are important, when I returned home I did not dwell on the suffering of those two days. I was strangely weak, really, and the word strange belongs here. The strangeness lay in the fact that although the shop window experience I have talked about held true for everything, it was most true for people and objects that particularly interested me. For instance, if I read a book that interested me, I read it with vivid pleasure, but my very pleasure was behind a pane of glass and unavailable to me because of that, but also far away and in an eternal past. Yet where unimportant people and things were involved, life regained its ordinary meaning and actuality, so that though I preferred to keep life at a distance, I had to seek it in simple actions and everyday people. That is why I worked, and always seemed more and more alive.

The night after my return home, as I was lying awake (sleep had left me at the same time as my blood), I heard my neighbor Colette crying violently; with occasional pauses the tears lasted for nearly two hours. This sorrow, in someone who did not seem very sensitive, awoke no sympathy in me: from time to time it disturbed me, because it went on for so long; but endless sorrow cannot move anyone. Still, the next day I made the effort to go see her. As soon as I opened the door, I felt there was something unexpected there, I saw disorder, clothes on the floor: well, I thought, this is misery, how strange it is. But the room was empty; I did not recognize the scattered clothes (even though, to tell the truth, I have since then imagined that I did recognize them). Back in my room, I thought with great surprise about the tears of the night before, so powerful, so violent, and about that impersonal sadness, the sadness of the other side of the wall, which I had not for one second hesitated to assume came from a certain person, with the presumption that is born of indifference, and which had not touched me then but which now overwhelmed me: this sadness communicated a feeling to me that was absolutely distressing, that was dispossessed and in some way bereft of itself; the memory of it became inexpressible despair, despair which hides in tears but does not cry, which has no face and changes the face it borrows into a mask. I telephoned the concierge and asked her, "Who on earth lives in the room next to mine?" Then I wrote to Nathalie (at her office) "I would like to see you. If you want to see me too, come to such-and-such a café, in the rue Royale, at such-and-such a time."

The night before, I had been on the point of dying. So it was with great difficulty that I drove there; N. said absolutely nothing, and for my part I looked at her fixedly, with a mean and sick look, without finding in her (though she was very charming) the slightest reason for this meeting. On top of that, she finally made this unfortunate remark: "Haven't you been very sick?" "Just come to the room," I said in the most menacing tone of voice. I imagine she came with me because of the irremediability of things. But once she was in the room again—even though the circumstances were entirely different—she was visibly seized by the same fear, the same confusion that had first struck her, except that this time she no longer even tried to leave. She stood still and I watched her from my bed. Physically she showed a trace of Slavic influence in the shape of her face, which had a certain thickness, and in the peculiarity of her eyes, which were dull, almost passive, but then suddenly of hallucinating brilliance, more than blue, of jewel-like ardor. Since I was as weak as I have described, I saw her from infinitely far away: she was before my eyes, which see everything, but still I asked myself this question: do I notice her at all? She certainly found herself wrestling with strange feelings, in the room. After all, she thought she had committed an evil act by coming here impulsively. But once here, she could not understand what was happening, she had the feeling that in order to understand she would have to be outside, and once outside, things would perhaps have changed radically. I am summarizing what she wrote to me about it, because though she talked very little she found it easy to write.

I think I can state positively that she said only one thing, but that one thing was strangely bold. In the midst of the silence she asked me, "Do you know other women?" "Yes, of course." A fairly clear meaning can be ascribed to this question. That meaning, I am sure, would be ridiculously misleading, or at least so straight-forward, so simple that it would represent nothing of the truth which was touched upon there; and even my answer, in its spontaneity, meant something that had nothing to do with life and the course of the world. I have never been frank. I have never thought that just because you happen to meet many people, you are obliged to surrender them to the curiosity or the jealousy of other people: they appear and disappear in an obscurity which they merit. My frankness was therefore a new right, a warning given in the name of a truth which did not require any ordinary proofs and which emerged from hidden things to assert itself proudly in my mouth.

Nathalie was not at all innocent: she too had met people. During her childhood, in a foreign country, she had lived across from a monastery, a majestic building lost in an estate full of trees and surrounded by a high wall. She was completely preoccupied by what went on behind that wall. One day she heard terrifying cries coming from there, loud, solitary and imploring cries, the sort one can imagine hearing in an insane asylum. From then on the monastery became, for her, a prison for madmen, and the idea formed in her mind that as soon as there was any place she could not enter, after having wanted to enter it, then madness or at least painful and miserable things would come out of it to attack her. She was therefore always a little tempted to anticipate her desires, not because they were important to her, but in order to prevent them from becoming important. I write that because she wrote it to me, certainly not in order to endow her with a particular character; I do not know what her character is, I do not know if she has one.

To show that in the most serious situations beginnings do not matter, I will tell why, according to her, she had the idea of coming to my room that day: she was on the point of committing herself to someone. Since she had been married, but had broken up her marriage, and had always led a very free life too, I do not see how this new step necessarily would have driven her towards a place I had disappeared from. But in any case, at that moment she wanted to make up her mind. So she came into this room, and what did she meet up with here? From me, the motions of a madman who did not recognize her; for her, a feeling of dread which had forced her outside with the thought that she had seen something she had no right to see, so that my name was the one she would most happily have banished from her memory. I will add that when she answered the question I asked—"Why have you come?"—by saying, "I've forgotten," that answer was much more exact and more important (in my opinion) than the one this story holds.

At a certain point in my life I struggled stubbornly against a person I did not want to meet. I was persisting resolutely in this struggle, but I was watching it at the same time. Seeing many hidden motives in this fight, I took responsibility for them in a spirit of clearsightedness and recognized that my feelings were rather ambiguous. But it was there that my weakness lay—not in the fight itself, which sought only one outcome, but in my misguided lucidity, which made me assume that it had a different outcome and denounce its intentions. For example, events would bring us together in the same foreign city. It would only be a matter of good or bad luck. But if I saw in it the least shadow of calculation I immediately made possible the incidents which drew us toward one another in that city, incidents which never would have taken place if I had not disturbed my good faith. What, then, blinded me? My clearsightedness. What misled me? My straightforward spirit. What makes it happen that every time my grave opens, now, I rouse a thought there that is strong enough to bring me back to life? The very derisive laughter of my death.

But know this, that where I am going there is neither work, nor wisdom, nor desire, nor struggle; what I am entering, no one enters. That is the meaning of the last fight.

After I said "Yes, of course," something bad happened to N. That overheated room where I was dying of cold suddenly became a freezing place for her, too. She began to tremble, her teeth chattered, and for a moment she shivered so violently that she lost control of her body. It horrified me to see the cold assaulting her. I could do nothing to help her; by approaching her, by talking to her, I was disobeying the law; by touching her, I could have killed her. To struggle alone, to learn, as she struggled, how through the workings of a profound justice the greatest adverse forces console us and upraise us, at the very moment they are tearing us apart: that is what she had to do. But it seems to me that I may have dreaded something horrible: at one moment, that horror was almost there. The needle is moving forward, I thought, after she had gone.

Still unable to sleep, I spent part of the night looking at the armchair, which was quite far from the bed but turned towards me. Neither light nor darkness have ever bothered me. A persistent thought is completely beyond the reach of its conditions. What has sometimes impressed me about this thought is a sort of hardness, the infinite distance between its respect for me and my respect for it; but hardness is not a fair word: the hardness arose from me, from my own person. I can even imagine this: that if I had walked by its side more often in those days, as I do now, if I had granted it the right to sit down at my table, and to lie down next to me, instead of living intimately with it for several seconds during which all its proud powers were revealed, and during which my own powers seized it with an even greater pride, then we would not have lacked familiarity, nor equality in sadness, nor absolute frankness, and perhaps I would have known something about its intentions which even it could never have known, made so cold by my distance that it was put under glass, prey to one obstinate dream.

After I had spent part of that night in a painful state — I was still very sick, and there remained of my poisoning brief bouts of nausea during which there were sort of cold avalanches, a sickening collapse of empty images — I told myself I would not go out of that room anymore, nor would anyone enter it, that it was cowardly of me to open it halfway on the outdoors, that what I had said—"Yes, of course"—was one speech too many and no one would ever hear it again. (The night had not dispelled N.'s perfume: I could still smell it very clearly.) The next day I took a room in another hotel, though I kept this one. I lived that way as long as I had the means to, sometimes in three or four different places. At the beginning of the war, the idea of renting a room in an apartment that other people lived in led me to the home of a woman who gave dancing lessons. This woman had a daughter thirteen or fourteen years old who spent hours spying on me through the transom of a small parlor that adjoined my room. She would climb up on a chair and watch me with a dazed look on her face. In the beginning, when I took her by surprise, she would hide; but soon she chose to remain in sight. This sly behavior of hers did not make me angry. To see her head up there all the time, that head which seemed alone and poised in empty space, gave me a feeling of calm. But one day, as I came in through the little parlor, I saw her on the chair looking into my room even when I was not there. I slapped her and took her to her mother, saying, "Whenever a woman comes to see me this girl gets up on a chair and looks through the window." Her mother was stupefied. After a minute she said, "But you shouldn't be bringing women here." To be precise, I did not "bring" women there; I only wanted to make her understand the kind of indiscretion her daughter had committed by looking into my room when I was not home.

When I think about it carefully, the change which appeared in Nathalie, after what happened to her, was not evident to me at first, because I myself was changing, and that was unfortunate. I talked about this earlier. An empty movement threw me into each instant; it was my blood that was playing this dirty trick on me and giving me, an animal with very cool blood, all the nervous irritation of an animal with feverish blood. On top of this, I was extremely busy. I can say that by getting involved with Nathalie I was hardly getting involved with anyone: that is not meant to belittle her; on the contrary, it is the most serious thing I can say about a person. But at that time, I saw her most of all as someone charming who was just as free as I was. I went to see her in a sort of run-down attic where she lived alone with her little girl. It seems to me it was an immense place, with an infinite number of rooms; except that they were not rooms but closets, nooks, bits of hallway, all of this more or less empty and neglected. I was only allowed to go into one small room, doubtless the only habitable one. Yet in my mind there is the image of a large rotunda, quite beautiful and well kept up, but perhaps in another building. Nathalie worked; she translated writings from all sorts of different languages, at least from German, English, and Russian. That was an aspect of her character which helped to mislead me about her. For me, the fact that she worked in an office, that she dealt with printed papers, that she accomplished her tasks, put her back in that daily life which I had often required to be merely pleasant, without any ulterior motives, as if, at that very time, I had not spent my nights in an open grave. Still, I cannot say that she was only one face among many; she was less than all the others, that was her peculiar quality, and this quality of being less, when I think about it, is a truly strange anomaly, a surprising and distressing phenomenon, which would have told me something if I had been sensitive to it and yet which I sometimes caught sight of, as I thought about that rare person whom I was neglecting for so many other people. Infidelity may be good, or it may be bad; I am not passing judgment on it: but its merit—as far as earthly things are concerned—is to keep the story in reserve, as it prepares a feeling which will burst into view when it has lost all its rights.

I had been anxious to see her after this "accident," and I had gone up to her attic. I think no one was more incapable of coquetry, I mean purposely indecisive behavior and ambivalent talk. When she saw me there, she suddenly suggested of her own accord, very self-conscious and without any secret purpose, that I come live in that immense place. In some way this offer followed from the bold things she had said in my room. So that someone in her was continuing to act with a strange end in view and in ways likely to deceive me. My answer, much less serious than the first one, since I was becoming blind to things, was a refusal, enveloped in words and slightly insolent. I was protecting myself from her a little, as though I were in the presence of someone who had threatened my freedom. Besides, I clearly saw the innocence of that offer, but I did not see the ambiguous feelings at the heart of this innocence. She made no remark about this refusal and began playing her role of being no one. With her, everything seemed astonishingly easy. I met her at one place or another, we had dinner, I drove her home. One day she caught sight of me from a distance (she was working for the Ministry of Information then) in one of the immense corridors of the building that housed the Ministry: she saw me waiting. But the idea that she was the person I was waiting for did not occur to her, as though we had not been friends at all, and whenever I seemed to be looking at another woman in an intimate way, she always remained less than a person, neither upset, nor angry, nor curious. One time, though, she narrowed her eyes in a peculiar way; I said to her afterwards: "Your eyes aren't always pleased with me." But something truly astounding was that she no more thought of denying this agitation than of getting angry with herself for having revealed it or with me for having caused it by my bad manners. So she seemed incapable of wanting to hide a feeling behind her feelings. She had said to me twice, with the most simple frankness, that she was perfectly happy when I was there. But nothing allowed me to see what happened when I was not there.

At the moment I forget several scenes in which she was completely different. And this forgetting shows how much more I was able to forget them at the time. One of them, as far as I remember, took place towards the beginning. Whenever I went there, her little girl was shut up or else had gone to bed, so I rarely saw her. This little girl got her own way in everything, that was the rule, she could do what she liked; Nathalie's in-laws, who took care of her most of the time, must have given in about this, in spite of the scandalousness of such a crazy upbringing. No doubt little Christiana had her own opinion of this visitor, who was the only one to expose her to such unusual discipline, although properly speaking it was not discipline, since she was only immediately asked to stay away from the little room. Well, it might seem surprising, but Christiana always respected this rule and if she came, it was after having ceremoniously requested an interview by way of her mother, which proves that this upbringing was not so crazy. One evening, however, perhaps because she was afraid, she left her bed and ran to the little room; I was very pleased to see her, but Nathalie's anger was terrible. She ended up giving her a little wound on the lip with her ring. This act was so extraordinary that although I generally asked her questions about everything, I never dared talk to her about it.

A long time after that scene, she went on a trip to take Christiana to the country. It was very difficult to know what she felt about her daughter. Anyone would have thought she adored her: she sacrificed a thousand precious things for her; she spent hours taking care of her; though her eyes would be tired and though she hated to read, she would read book after book out loud to please her. But she said to me over and over again: "I would willingly grow ten years older and give those ten years to Christiana so that she would be old enough to look to someone else." It is strange, too, that for so long she was opposed to teaching her music. She herself had been taught it by a governess who came to her parents' house. Her older brother was having an affair with this governess, a French student who was easily bored by her studies. N. said that she did not like her brother, but liked the governess a great deal more, and the jealousy aroused in her by these meetings, which always took place at the time of the lessons, completely clouded her mind, so that she learned nothing. So that her mother would not suspect anything, she was forced to play the piano without stopping and very loudly during these intervals. The mystery was how, in spite of this, she was able to become a pianist who played well, who played at least certain pieces well, because there were many that she could neither play nor listen to; for example, she detested Mozart with an incomprehensible hatred. As for Christiana, she swore that she had neither ear, nor voice, nor good hands, which was somewhat true, but not entirely true. One would have thought that for some mysterious reason she wanted to keep her away from the piano at all costs. I said to her: "I'm going to try to give her lessons." I gave her a few, and she took over from me.

On the morning of her departure, she telephoned and asked to see me for a few minutes, which for her was a big initiative. The truth was that I could have come, but did not want to very much. So I gave her a rather unkind answer. Her own answer was an impressive silence, a silence which upset me, which put me in the wrong, and finally I asked her: "Where do you want me to meet you?" "Nowhere." This was said in the most agitated tone of voice; it was a sort of frenzied cry which would not have seemed natural to me even coming from the most violent sort of person. Sometimes I brooded over that "Nowhere."

The last incident was quite different. These outbursts were always unusual and were immediately forgotten. She underwent a minor operation on her eye, made necessary partly by her weak vision, vision which was even abnormal, because in the daytime she saw fairly well, while at night, under artificial light, she could hardly see at all. She assured me that the operation was not serious, and it is true that she did not have to stay at the clinic very long. I also thought that she did not want to be seen with a bandage over her eyes. This time my fault had more serious causes. I could not associate illness with her name. Now I see the reasons for that. But even then I understood quite clearly why something jealous arose in me, a dark torment, a resentment, at the thought of that clinic bed and of a free body which was made both important and non-existent by this serious business of illness. So I did not go to see her. The operation came off very well. Once she was home, I did not go there either—a neglect for which there was no excuse, though there was a pretext. It happened that on the evening chosen for our meeting, I had to go to the theater for reasons connected with my work, and could only tell her at the last minute: she gave me a very kind answer. At the theater, during the intermission, I saw her with a young man I did not know. She seemed very beautiful to me. I saw her passing in front of me, walking back and forth in a place that was very near and infinitely separated from me, as if it were behind a window. I was struck by an insane idea. No doubt I could have talked to her, but I did not want to and maybe I actually was not able to. She remained in my presence with the freedom of a thought; she was in this world, but I was encountering her again in this world only because she was my thought; and what tacit understanding was therefore being established between her and my thought, what terrifying complicity. I must add that she looked at me like someone who knew me very well and even regarded me in a friendly way, but it was a recognition from behind the eyes, without a look and without a sign, a recognition of thought, friendly, cold and dead.

Was this a fleeting impression? It seems to me that it tore my life apart, that from that moment on, I had almost nothing left to learn, and yet, if I look at what I did and how I lived, nothing had changed either; with her, I was neither better nor worse, and she always put up with my presence and my absence equally well. Yet I must recall what was happening. It became more and more serious: thinking and living did not go hand in hand anymore. But if at that time I made an effort—which failed—to enter into the conflict in a more real way, I could not swear that the anxiety of the nation had nothing to do with it, but it is much more true that I sought in the madness of blood and arms hope of escaping the inevitable.

Since we happened to be in the street at the moment Paris was bombed, we had to take shelter in the metro. At that time these formalities were not taken seriously. And N. enjoyed anything that allowed her to leave her work. So the two of us were on the steps in the middle of an enormous crowd, the kind of crowd that is urgent and unwieldly, sometimes as motionless as the earth, sometimes rushing down like a torrent. For quite some time I had been talking to her in her mother tongue, which I found all the more moving since I knew very few words of it. As for her, she never actually spoke it, at least not with me, and yet if I began to falter, to string together awkward expressions, to form impossible idioms, she would listen to them with a kind of gaiety, and youth, and in turn would answer me in French, but in a different French from her own, more childish and talkative, as though her speech had become irresponsible, like mine, using an unknown language. And it is true that I too felt irresponsible in this other language, so unfamiliar to me; and this unreal stammering, of expressions that were more or less invented, and whose meaning flitted past, far away from my mind, drew from me things I never would have said, or thought, or even left unsaid in real words: it tempted me to let them be heard, and imparted to me, as I expressed them, a slight drunkenness which was no longer aware of its limits and boldly went farther than it should have. So I made the most friendly declarations to her in this language, which was a habit quite alien to me. I offered to marry her at least twice, which proved how fictitious my words were, since I had an aversion to marriage (and little respect for it), but in her language I married her, and I not only used that language lightly but, more or less inventing it, and with the ingenuity and truth of half-awareness, I expressed in it unknown feelings which shamelessly welled up in the form of that language and fooleɑ even me, as they could have fooled her.

They did not fool her at all; I am sure of that. And perhaps my frivolity, though it made her a little frivolous too, aroused disagreeable thoughts more than anything else, not to speak of one other thought about which I cannot say anything. Even now, when so many things have become clear, it is difficult for me to imagine what the word marriage could have awoken in her. She had once been married, but that business had left her only the memory of the unpleasant details of the divorce. So that marriage was not very important to her either. And yet why was it that the only time, or one of the only times, she answered me in her own language, was after I had proposed marriage to her: the word was a strange one, completely unknown to me, which she never wanted to translate for me, and when I said to her: "All right, then I'm going to translate it," she was seized by real panic at the thought that I might hit on it exactly, so that I had to keep both my translation and my presentiment to myself.

It is possible that the idea of being married to me seemed like a very bad thing to her, a sort of sacrilege, or quite the opposite, a real happiness, or finally, a meaningless joke. Even now, I am almost incapable of choosing among these interpretations. Enough of this. As I said, I was deluding myself much more than I was her with these words, which spoke within me in the language of someone else. I said too much about it to her not to feel what I was saying; inwardly I committed myself to honoring these strange words; the more extreme they were, I mean alien to what might have been expected of me, the more true they seemed to me because they were novel, because they had no precedent; the more I wanted, since they could not be believed, to make them believable, even to myself, especially to myself, putting all my effort into going farther and farther and building, on what might have been a rather narrow foundation, a pyramid so dizzying that its ever growing height dumbfounded even me. Still, I can put this down in writing: it was true; there cannot be any illusions when such great excesses are involved. My mistake in this situation, the temptations of which I see most clearly, was much more the result of the distance I imagined I was maintaining from her by these completely imaginary ways of drawing close to her. Actually, all that, which began with words I did not know and led me to see her much more often, to call her again and again, to want to convince her, to force her to see something other than a language in my language, also urged me to look for her at an infinite distance, and contributed so naturally to her air of absence and strangeness that I thought it was sufficiently explained by this, and that as I was more and more attracted by it,

I was less and less aware of its abnormal nature and its terrible source.

No doubt I went extremely far, the day we took shelter in the metro. It seems to me that I was driven by something wild, a truth so violent that I suddenly broke down all the frail supports of that language and began speaking French, using insane words that I had never dreamt of using before and that fell on her with all the power of their madness. Hardly had they touched her when I was physically aware that something was being shattered. Just at that moment she was swept away from me, borne off by the crowd, and as it hurled me far away, the unchained spirit of that crowd struck me, battered me, as if my crime had turned into a mob and was determined to separate us forever.

I had no news of her during the afternoon (the incident had taken place at about two o'clock). I was working, and the hazards of work are excuse enough for any evasion. I said to myself: if I don't know anything by eight o'clock this evening, I will be mortally uneasy; which quieted my uneasiness for a little while. At the Ministry, no one had seen her, but no one saw anyone at the Ministry. At eight o'clock I looked for her in those empty corridors, and in those offices that were full of people and empty. I looked for her in a little restaurant and I was obliged to have dinner there in order to wait for her. At her house, no one had answered the telephone. Nevertheless, I went there, thinking that she was not answering it. That idea reassured me, I was really certain I would find her in that little room: every time I had gone, she had been there. But the door, which was absolutely deaf, was my worst enemy: if it had been open, I would have put up with the deserted apartment; I would have been able to make out the trail she had left in passing through; I would have had a place where I could wait for her, I would have replaced her by my presence and forced her to come by the obstinacy of my waiting for her. How bitterly I thought of my refusal to live there. And I cursed Christiana for being in the country, where she could not stop her mother from getting lost. At that moment, I was lost myself. My madness no longer arose from my uneasiness nor from my concern for Nathalie, but from an impatience which grew with each passing minute and which went beyond any purpose, turning me into a wanderer in search of nothing. I returned to the neighborhood of the Ministry. I was acting on the idea that if she was to be found anywhere, it would be near the river: an idea which appealed to me only because it was unreasonable, since Natalie was disgusted by suicide. I stayed there for an infinitely long time. I recall nothing about that person who spent so many hours on a bridge. The night, it seems to me, was impenetrable.

At a certain moment, the uneasiness disappeared completely and reason returned to me, at least a fairly cool and lucid feeling which said to me: the time has come, now you have to do what has to be done. I was living in a hotel in the rue S.; I still had the room in the other hotel, but since the landlord had been called up and the hotel was nearly empty, I had nothing there but some books and I almost never went there; I did not go there at night unless it was really necessary. I did not like the hotel in rue S., which was roomy and comfortable. Because of a whim which I do not understand, I had asked N. never to go there; one morning she had called me there and as I talked to her my bad temper had been so intense that even now I hate that place because of what I said. I felt incapable of spending the night there. The strange thing was that I never thought she might be waiting for me there; I did not even look in the lobby, nor in the lounge, where Central European diplomats engaged in endless conversations, heaping up the greatest visions of unhappiness. I went to ask for a room in a rather shady hotel in the next street, but there were no more rooms available there. I crossed rue de la Paix, which was extraordinarily quiet, and without light. How quiet it was, and how tranquil I was, too. I could hear my footsteps. Rue d'O. was not quiet, but gloomy; the elevator was not working and in the stairwell, from the fourth floor on up, a sort of strange musty smell came down to me, a cold smell of earth and stone which I was perfectly familiar with because in the room it was my very life. I always carried the key with me, and as a precaution I carried it in a wallet. Imagine that stairwell plunged in darkness, where I was groping my way up. Two steps from the door I had a shock: the key was no longer there. My fear had always been that I would lose that key. Often, during the day, I would search my wallet for it; it was a little key, a Yale key, I knew every detail of it. This loss brought back all my anxiety in an instant, and it had been augmented by such a powerful certainty of un-happiness that I had that unhappiness in my mouth and the taste of it has remained there ever since. I was not thinking anymore. I was behind that door. This might seem ridiculous, but I think I begged it, entreated it, I think I cursed it, but when it did not respond, I did something which can only be explained by my lack of self-control: I struck it violently with my fist, and it opened immediately.

I will say very little about what happened then: what

happened had already happened long ago, or for a long time had been so imminent that not to have revealed it, when I felt it every night of my life, is a sign of my secret understanding with this premonition. I did not have to take another step to know that there was someone in that room. That if I went forward, all of a sudden someone would be there in front of me, pressing up against me, absolutely near me, of a proximity that people are not aware of: I knew that too. Everything about that room, plunged in the most profound darkness, was familiar to me; I had penetrated it, I carried it in me, I gave it life, a life which is not life, but which is stronger than life and which no force in the world could ever overcome. That room does not breathe, there is neither shadow nor memory in it, neither dream nor depth; I listen to it and no one speaks; I look at it and no one lives in it. And yet, the most intense life is there, a life which I touch and which touches me, absolutely similar to others, which clasps my body with its body, marks my mouth with its mouth, whose eyes open, whose eyes are the most alive, the most profound eyes in the world, and whose eyes see me. May the person who does not understand that come and die. Because that life transforms the life which shrinks away from it into a falsehood.

I went in; I closed the door. I sat down on the bed. Blackest space extended before me. I was not in this blackness, but at the edge of it, and I confess that it is terrifying. It is terrifying because there is something in it which scorns man and which man cannot endure without losing himself. But he must lose himself; and whoever resists will founder, and whoever goes forward will become this very blackness, this cold and dead and scornful thing in the very heart of which lives the infinite. This blackness stayed next to me, probably because of my fear: this fear was not the fear people know about, it did not break me, it did not pay any attention to me, but wandered around the room the way human things do. A great deal of patience is required if thought, when it has been driven down into the depths of the horrible, is to rise little by little and recognize us and look at us. But I still dreaded that look. A look is very different from what one might think, it has neither light nor expression nor force nor movement, it is silent, but from the heart of the strangeness its silence crosses worlds and the person who hears that silence is changed. All of a sudden the certainty that someone was there who had come to find me became so intense that I drew back from her, knocked violently into the bed, and immediately saw her distinctly, three or four paces from me, that dead and empty flame in her eyes. I had to stare at her, with all my strength, and she stared at me, but in a strange way, as if I had been in back of myself, and infinitely far back. Perhaps that went on for a very long time, even though my impression is that she had hardly found me before I lost her. At any rate, I remained in that place for a very long time without moving. I was no longer at all afraid for myself, but for her I was extremely afraid, of alarming her, of transforming her, through fear, into a wild thing which would break in my hands. I think I was aware of that fear, and yet it also seems to me that everything was so entirely calm that I could have sworn there was nothing in front of me. It was probably because of that calm that I moved forward a little, I moved forward in the slowest possible way, I brushed against the fireplace, I stopped; I recognized in myself such great patience, such great respect for that solitary night that I made almost no movement; only my hand went forward a little, but with great caution, so as not to frighten. I wanted most of all to go towards the armchair, I saw that armchair in my mind, it was there, I was touching it. In the end I got to my knees so that I would not be too large, and my hand slowly crossed through the dark, brushed against the wooden back of the chair, brushed against some cloth: there had never been a more patient hand, nor one more calm, nor more friendly; that is why it did not tremble when another hand, a cold hand, slowly formed beside it, and that hand, so still and so cold, allowed mine to rest on it without trembling. I did not move, I was still on my knees, all this was taking place at an infinite distance, my own hand on this cold body seemed so far away from me, I saw myself so widely separated from it, and pushed back by it into something desperate which was life, that all my hope seemed to me infinitely far away, in that cold world where my hand rested on this body and loved it and where this body, in its night of stone, welcomed, recognized and loved that hand.

Perhaps this lasted several minutes, perhaps an hour. I put my arms around her, I was completely motionless and she was completely motionless. But a moment came when I saw that she was still mortally cold, and I drew closer and said to her: "Come." I got up and took her by the hand; she got up too and I saw how tall she was. She walked with me, and all her movements had the same docility as mine. I made her lie down; I lay down next to her. I took her head between my hands and said to her, as gently as I could, "Look at me." Her head actually did rise between my hands and immediately I saw her again three or four paces from me, that dead and empty flame in her eyes. With all my strength,

I stared at her, and she too seemed to stare at me, but infinitely far behind me. Then something awoke in me, I leaned over her and said, "Now don't be afraid, I'm going to blow on your face." But as I came near her she moved very quickly and drew away (or pushed me back).

I would like to say that the coldness of these bodies is something very strange: in itself, it is not so intense. When I touch a hand, as I am doing now, when my hand lies under this hand, this hand is not as icy as mine is; but this little bit of cold is profound; it is not a slight radiation from the surface, but penetrates, envelopes, one must follow it and with it enter an unlimited thickness, an empty and unreal depth where there is no possible return to contact with the outside. That is what makes it so bitter: it seems to have the cruelty of something that gnaws at you, that catches hold of you and entices you, and it actually does catch hold of you, but that is also its secret, and one who has enough sympathy to abandon himself to this coldness finds in it the kindness, the tenderness, and the freedom of a real life. It must be said, because it would certainly be useless to shrink from it now: the coldness of a hand, the coldness of a body is nothing, and even if the lips draw near it, the bitterness of that cold mouth is only frightening to someone who can be neither more bitter nor more cold, but there is another barrier which separates us: the lifeless material on a silent body, the clothes which must be acknowledged and which clothe nothing, steeped in insensitivity, with their cadaverous folds and their metallic inertness. This is the obstacle which must be overcome.

In the morning, when I saw her in this room again, she was quite cheerful. After looking at her hands and her fingernails, which were always well cared for, she said right away, but with good humor, "Look, I'm behaving like a child, I think I've been biting my nails." Later she discovered a little cut at the top of her forehead, under her hair. With infinite emotion, I watched her get up and walk around in that room. I was not thinking about anything; I was entirely taken up with the pleasure of watching her, of watching her make the slightest gesture, the slightest movement. I was determined to ignore my work and hers completely, so that, each minute, she would remain before my eyes.

She resisted this idea a little, but only a little. Anyway, she enjoyed not working. As we went out, I felt a pang of uneasiness, and I could not stop myself from saying to her, "I think you have the key." She took that little key out of her purse in the most natural way and when the door had been closed tossed it back into the purse. Why would I have questioned her at that moment? Such an incredible act on her part, the impulse which had made her deliberately take my wallet from me, put her hand in that wallet, and take hold of the key, could have no justification in this world, and in the same way any questions I might ask seemed to me just as indiscreet as anything I could have reproached her for. If bad luck has it that a person whom one sets above everything and whom one loves more than anything else reads a letter which is not meant for him, it is necessary to be ignorant of it, not to forget it, but if one knows about it, never to know about it, and if one suspects it, to make that frightful incident impossible, by an absolute faith in truth and loyalty—and in fact that incident becomes ashamed of itself and soon withers away to nothing.

If I had questioned N., she would have said, "Yes, I took the key." And if I had asked her, Why did you do it, what she would have answered me without hesitating, what I was sure she was always ready to say in answer, was of such a nature that neither she nor I could have gone on living those hours and those days in a natural manner. Well, I no longer wanted anything but this: I wanted to come in here with her, into a certain café, or enter the tedium of a certain movie theater, hear something laugh, in her, which would signify only frivolous vanity; above all, I wanted to keep the name Nathalie forever, even at the price of her bitten nails and her cut forehead.

I do not see why those hours and those days should not have been extremely happy. I acted in such a way, moved by such emotion and such affection, that I did not have time to feel anything else but the truth of that emotion and the strength of that affection. The fact that N. was often very reserved did not impress itself on me as though I were missing something, but my own lack of reserve grew because of it, and in my own fever and my own passion, which were more and more exacting, I took for a similarly feverish transport her manner of tolerating from a distance my boundless eagerness to spend time together. Besides, it is certain that she was extremely attached to me, and she was becoming more so every day: but what does the word attachment refer to? And the word passion—what does it mean? And the word ecstasy? Who has experienced the most intense feeling? Only I have, and I know that it is the most glacial of all, because it has triumphed over an immense defeat, and is even now triumphing over it, and at each instant, and always, so that time no longer exists for it.

Naturally, what I had to do was live with her, in her apartment: I had to take my revenge on that door. I went everywhere in the immense loft, everywhere I thought she might be. I did not follow her like a shadow, because a shadow disappears at times, but though she was free at every step, doing everything she wanted to, her liberty still went by way of my own, and if she was alone for an instant, she would find me there even more, because of all the endless questions she knew I would ask her about that instant and about all the other instants when she was living alone. Everyone knows that I talk very little. But at certain times I was driven to talk by a force so compelling, I felt determined to transform the most simple details of life into so many insignificant words, that my voice, which was becoming the only space where I allowed her to live, forced her to emerge from her silence too, and gave her a sort of physical certainty, a physical solidity, which she would not have had otherwise. All this may seem childish. It does not matter. This childishness was powerful enough to prolong an illusion that had already been lost, and to force something to be there which was no longer there. It seems to me that in all this incessant talking there was the gravity of one single word, the echo of that "Come" which I had said to her; and she had come, and she would never be able to go away again.

About a week after that day, a friend involved me in something which I will not talk about in detail, since it does not concern me. What I can say about it is that he was going to fight a duel if I did not succeed in persuading his antagonist, who did not know me any better than I knew him, to be a little reasonable, and the questions that had to be cleared up were of the most intimate kind. This business, which seemed all the more insane because of the general confusion, occupied me for nearly a whole day. I went from one person to the other and reported what had been said, misrepresenting it though I had sworn to convey it in the most faithful way; towards the end of the afternoon I went to the girl's home to give her some papers, and in exchange she gave me some objects. At a time like that, these incidents seemed to me like the last grimace of the world. But this friend felt that the affair was extremely serious, and I liked him.

Perhaps it was a mistake to do this—and besides, all these circumstances and my interpretations of them are only a way for me to remain a little longer in the realm of things which can be told and experienced—my mistake, and it was a glaring one, was to act according to other people's standards. I felt pledged to secrecy and I said only a few vague words to N. about this affair, which had kept me away the whole day. I must emphasize that my discretion was not honorable. Such lack of frankness only meant that after a day devoted to what other people conceived of as honor, I was still completely impregnated with the way of life and the attitude of other people, that is to say I was unfaithful to a way of life and an attitude that were much more important. What do I care about that honor, or even that friend, or even his unhappiness? My own is immense, and next to it other people mean nothing.

One should not have faith in dramatic decisions. There was no drama anywhere. In me it had in one second become weaker, slightly distracted, less real. And the most terrible thing is that in those minutes I was aware of the insane price I was going to pay for an instant of distraction, I knew that if I did not immediately again become a man carried away by an unbridled feeling I was in danger of losing both a life and the other side of a life. This idea was clearly present in me, and I had only to overcome a little fatigue, but it was the fatigue which was whispering this idea to me, and while I thought about it I became more and more false and cold.

At about ten o'clock Nathalie said to me:

"I telephoned X., I asked him to make a cast of my head and my hands."

Right away I was seized by a feeling of terror. "What gave you the idea of doing that?" "The card." She showed me a sculptor's card which was usually with the key in my wallet. "It seems to me you don't always behave very sensibly with that wallet." "Why?" That why implied such forgetfulness of things that my other feelings were consumed by anxiety. "I beg you, give up that idea." She shook her head. "I can't," she said sadly. "You can't? Why not?" I hung on her answer, but such great sadness lay in her eyes, something so motionless and so cold, that my question remained suspended between us and I would have liked to hold it up, to raise it to her face, so strongly did I feel that she would no longer accept it. What I had to do was to come out of myself truly, and with my life give life to these words. But I was weak, what weakness, what miserable impotence. In the face of her muteness I returned to myself, I who had perhaps talked to her about X., perhaps described the process: a process which is strange when it is carried out on living people, sometimes dangerous, surprising, a process which... Abruptly, anger burned me: "If you don't answer me," I cried, "I'll never speak to you again." A threat stupid enough to make the walls tremble, but which seemed to stop short in front of her. She looked at me ponderously, amicably, with a strange immobility. Why, she is meeting my eyes, I thought: usually she preferred to look at me when I was not watching her.

As gently as possible, I asked her:

"Are you listening to me?"

"Yes."

"Will you give up your plan or not?"

She looked at me with a look which I thought was almost willing.

"Say yes," and I took her by the hand to encourage her. "Otherwise I might just lock you up in this room."

"Where is that?"

"Why, here, in the house."

She listened for a minute, then she asked, "With you?" I nodded. I was still holding her hand, that hand which was alive gave me hope. Of her own accord she finally spoke:

"What was the word you said?"

I searched her face. My God, I said to myself absurdly, remind me of that word.

"What word?" I asked with a slight, promising smile.

I felt two things: that she was not smiling at all, but that even so the idea was still there.

"Just a minute ago," she murmured, her mind apparently fixed on the moment when my mouth opened to say it.

"Well," I began. But remembering "this room" I stopped short: yes, that was probably it. She must have been able to read the agitation in my face, because her hand squeezed mine with an encouragement so persuasive and so intelligent that my coolness deserted me. We looked at one another: how much hope I still had; what a treacherous, bad thing hope is. Little by little her look became smooth again. Because of her weak vision, I would often talk to her about her eyes, which were sometimes passive and empty, and sometimes inflamed by a burning of which only the disquieting reflection was visible. "Do your eyes hurt?" Altogether unexpectedly, this question seemed to stagger her; she got up, and passed her hands through her hair, as she always did in moments of great emotion. She was standing, almost against me, I wanted to take her arm, but she was not paying any attention to my person, which had suddenly been flung extremely far away. Yet I made her sit down. Slowly I put my hand on hers; this contact was like a bitter memory, an idea, a cold, implacable truth, and to fight against this truth could only be a shabby thing. At one moment I saw her lips move and was aware that she was talking, but now I, in turn, no longer made an effort to grasp those words: I looked at them. By chance, I heard the word "plan."

"That's the word," she said.

The memory of what she had been searching for returned to me then, but I must say that even though I was awake and attentive again I was no longer in the least interested; all that belonged to another world, in any case it was too late. Only, as often happens, my lack of interest must have brought her back to life and now, perhaps also because she had broken through a barrier, it was she who took the initiative.

"It isn't a plan any longer," she said timidly.

I understood her very well, her tone of voice was exactly like that of a child who has done something rather bad. Since I did not answer, she tried to find out whether I had understood her, and if I had not, how to think of words that were not too serious, to explain everything. She opened her hands in a gesture which, as I remember it, seems to me wonderfully innocent; then she asked in a weak voice:

"Shouldn't I have done it?"

I think meanness—which remains when everything

else is gone—made me shrug my shoulders, but the fact is that perhaps I was beginning to suffer again. She looked so human, she was still so close to me, waiting for a sort of absolution for that terrible thing which was certainly not her fault.

"It was probably necessary," I murmured.

She snatched at these words.

"It was necessary, wasn't it?"

It really seemed that my acquiescence reverberated in her, that it had been in some way expected, with an immense expectancy, by an invisible responsibility to which she lent only her voice, and that now a supreme power, sure of itself, and happy—not because of my consent, of course, which was quite useless to it, but because of its victory over life and also because of my loyal understanding, my unlimited abandon—took possession of this young person and gave her an acuity and a masterfulness that dictated my thoughts to me as well as my few words.

"Now," she said in a rather hoarse voice, "isn't it true that you've known about it all along?"

"Yes," I said, "I knew about it."

"And do you know when it happened?"

"I think I have some idea."

But my tone of voice, which must have been rather yielding and submissive, did not seem to satisfy her will to triumph.

"Well, maybe you don't know everything yet," she cried with a touch of defiance. And, really, within her jubilant exaltation there was a lucidity, a burning in the depths of her eyes, a glory which reached me through my distress, and touched me, too, with the same magnificent pride, the same madness of victory.

"Well, what?" I said, getting up too.

"Yes," she cried, "yes, yes!"

"That this took place a week ago?"

She took the words from my lips with frightening eagerness.

"And then?" she cried.

"And that today you went to X.'s to get...that thing?"

"And then!"

"And now that thing is over there, you have uncovered it, you have looked at it, and you have looked into the face of something that will be alive for all eternity, for your eternity and for mine! Yes, I know it, I know it, I've known it all along."

I cannot exactly say whether these words, or others like them, ever reached her ears, nor what mood led me to allow her to hear them: it was a minor matter, just as it was not important to know if things had really happened that way. But I must say that for me it seems that it did happen that way, setting aside the question of dates, since everything could have happened at a much earlier time. But the truth is not contained in these facts. I can imagine suppressing these particular ones. But if they did not happen, others happen in their place, and answering the summons of the all powerful affirmation which is united with me, they take on the same meaning and the story is the same. It could be that N., in talking to me about the "plan," wanted only to tear apart with a vigilant hand the pretences we were living under. It may be that she was tired of seeing me persevere with a kind of faith in my role as man of the "world," and that she used this story to recall me abruptly to my true condition and point out to me where my place was. It may also be that she herself was obeying a mysterious command, which came from me, and which is the voice that is always being reborn in me, and it is vigilant too, the voice of a feeling that cannot disappear. Who can say: this happened because certain events allowed it to happen? This occurred because, at a certain moment, the facts became misleading and because of their strange juxtaposition entitled the truth to take possession of them? As for me, I have not been the unfortunate messenger of a thought stronger than I, nor its plaything, nor its victim, because that *thought*, if it has conquered me, has only conquered through me, and in the end has always been equal to me. I have loved it and I have loved only it, and everything that happened I wanted to happen, and having had regard only for it, wherever it was or wherever I might have been, in absence, in unhappiness, in the inevitability of dead things, in the necessity of living things, in the fatigue of work, in the faces born of my curiosity, in my false words, in my deceitful vows, in silence and in the night, I gave it all my strength and it gave me all its strength, so that this strength is too great, it is incapable of being ruined by anything, and condemns us, perhaps, to immeasurable unhappiness, but if that is so, I take this unhappiness on myself and I am immeasurably glad of it and to that thought I say eternally, "Come," and eternally it is there.

These pages can end here, and nothing that follows what I have just written will make me add anything to it or take anything away from it. This remains, this will remain until the very end. Whoever would obliterate it from me, in exchange for that end which I am searching for in vain, would himself become the beginning of my own story, and he would be my victim. In darkness, he would see me: my word would be his silence, and he would think he was holding sway over the world, but that sovereignty would still be mine, his nothingness mine, and he too would know that there is no end for a man who wants to end alone.

This should therefore be impressed upon anyone who might read these pages thinking they are infused with the thought of unhappiness. And what is more, let him try to imagine the hand that is writing them: if he saw it, then perhaps reading would become a serious task for him.

Translator's Note

This translation follows the first edition of *L'Arrêt de Mort* (1948). In the second edition (1971), the brief final section was deleted by the author.

Design & production by
Patricia Nedds, George Quasha, & Susan Quasha.
Design consultation by Bruce McPherson.
Editorial consultation by Paul Auster & P. Adams Sitney.
Cover photograph by Jodi Rodar.

The text was set in Baskerville & printed on a Heidelberg KORD
at Open Studio in Rhinebeck, New York.